KABUL DISCO

NICOLAS WILD

KABUL DISCO

BOOK 1: HOW I MANAGED NOT TO BE ABDUCTED IN AFGHANISTAN

Life Drawn

V
an
KABULDIS
V.01

NICOLAS WILD
Story & Art

*

MARK BENCE
& FELICITY STILL
Translators

*

ALEX DONOGHUE
& FABRICE SAPOLSKY
U.S. Edition Editors

VINCENT HENRY
Original Edition Editor

JERRY FRISSEN
Senior Art Director

FABRICE GIGER
Publisher

Rights & Licensing - licensing@humanoids.com
Press and Social Media - pr@humanoids.com

KABUL DISCO: BOOK 1
This title is a publication of Humanoids, Inc. 8033 Sunset Blvd. #628, Los Angeles, CA 90046.
Copyright © 2018 Humanoids, Inc., Los Angeles (USA). All rights reserved. Humanoids and its logos are ® and © 2018 Humanoids, Inc.

Life Drawn is an imprint of Humanoids, Inc.

First published in France under the title "*Kaboul Disco Tome 1: Comment je ne me suis pas fait kidnapper en Afghanistan.*"
Copyright © 2007 La Boîte à Bulles & Nicolas Wild. All rights reserved. All characters, the distinctive likenesses thereof
and all related indicia are trademarks of La Boîte à Bulles Sarl and / or of Nicolas Wild.

YOU UP ALREADY?

NAH, I PULLED AN ALL-NIGHTER.

WAHOO! THAT'S MY 12TH COMIC BOOK DONE!

JUST GOTTA BURN IT ONTO A DVD AND ZAP IT OFF TO MY PUBLISHER...

AND WHAT ABOUT YOU, YA LAZYBONES? WHEN ARE YOU GETTING BACK INTO DRAWING COMICS?

CLING

DUNNO. NO IDEA. I'M WAITING FOR INSPIRATION TO KICK IN.

BIDOOP ♫ YOU GOT MAIL.

KICK IN? YOU NEED A KICK IN THE ASS!

AND HERE'S BOULET, THE *WITTIEST* GUY IN THE GALAXY!

GONNA FIX ME A QUICK COFFEE AND START ON MY 13TH BOOK!

FROM: CÉLINE SUBJECT: NONE NICOLAS, SAW THIS AD AND IMMEDIATELY THOUGHT OF YOU :-) HUGS...

AFGHAN COMMUNICATIONS AGENCY SEEKS COMIC ARTIST TO WORK IN KABUL. CONTACT VALENTIN SPIDAULT, ZENDAGUI MEDIA AND COMMUNICATION.

KABUL? YOU'D HAVE TO BE REALLY *DESPERATE* TO TAKE A JOB THERE...

BY THE WAY... MY REAL ROOMMATE'S COMING BACK NEXT WEEK. WHERE'RE YOU GONNA LIVE?

UH... I MIGHT HAVE FOUND A PLACE TO CRASH...

"MY REAL ROOMMATE"? SO WHAT DOES THAT MAKE ME? A SQUATTER?

TIP TAP TIP TAP

DEAR MR. SPIDAULT, MY NAME IS NICOLAS WILD AND I'D LIKE TO FIND OUT MORE ABOUT--

JUST GOT THE INTERNET AND ELECTRICITY BILLS... DID YOU TRANSFER YOUR PART OF THE RENT YET?

DEAR MR. SPIDAULT, MY NAME IS NICOLAS WILD AND, EVER SINCE I WAS LITTLE, I'VE HAD A BURNING PASSION FOR AFGHANISTAN...

TIP TAP TIP TIP TIP TAP TAP TAP TAP TIP TIP TAP TAP TIP TIP TAP

Part One
A WINTER IN KABUL

AND THAT'S HOW I ENDED UP IN...

...AZERBAIJAN.

NYET!

НИКАКЯ КОМНАТА НЕ ИДЕТ ПРОЧЬ!!

RECEPTION

DO YOU SPEAK ENGLISH?

NYET!

SPRECHEN SIE DEUTSCH?

NYET!

НИКАКЯ КОМНАТА НЕ ИДЕТ ПРОЧЬ!!

EXCUSE ME, YOUNG MAN, I THINK SHE'S SAYING THAT THE HOTEL IS FULL.

IF IT'S ANY HELP, YOU CAN SLEEP ON THE COUCH IN MY ROOM.

I WON'T SAY NO! I'M TOO BEAT TO LOOK ANYWHERE ELSE.

PRETTY FROSTY WELCOME...

IT'S LIKE SHE HASN'T HEARD THE COLD WAR'S OVER...

MY FLIGHT TO KABUL INCLUDED A FEW HOURS' STOPOVER IN BAKU, THE CAPITAL OF AZERBAIJAN...

BUT DUE TO WEATHER CONDITIONS, THE BAKU TO KABUL FLIGHT WAS CANCELED...

WINTERS ARE HARSH IN KABUL AND THE AIRPORT HAD NO EQUIPMENT TO CLEAR THE RUNWAY...

THE FLIGHT WAS THEN CANCELED THREE TIMES IN A ROW... I SPENT A WHOLE WEEK IN AZERBAIJAN...

DO YOU HAVE INTERNET?

NYET!

...A CHARMING COUNTRY RICH IN OIL AND POOR IN HUMAN RIGHTS.

THE GUY ON THE BILLBOARDS IS THEIR PRESIDENT. HE WON 80% OF THE VOTE...

THEY HAVE PIPELINES RIGHT IN THE CITY CENTER...

THE OLD CITY IS PRETTY...

THE SUBURBS ARE SOVIET...

THE CAVIAR'S SUBLIME...

DURING THE WEEK, THE HOTEL FILLED UP WITH TRAVELERS IN TRANSIT, ALL WAITING FOR THE ELUSIVE FLIGHT TO KABUL.

MIND IF I JOIN YOU?

ONE DISH ONLY

SO, AS I WAS SAYING... WE WERE STUCK IN THE LITTLE TUTSI VILLAGE FOR THREE WEEKS.

THE STREETS WERE LITTERED WITH WOMEN'S CORPSES AND CHILDREN'S HEADS.

THE HUTU MILITIAS COULD HAVE RETURNED ANY MINUTE...

MY GOD, I DON'T KNOW WHAT I'D DO IF I SAW A SEVERED HEAD...

AFTER THE FIRST FEW, YOU GET BLASÉ ABOUT IT.

WERE YOU OUT IN RWANDA TOO, MR. LIVA?

NO, I WAS IN YUGOSLAVIA...

AND YOU, NICOLAS? WHAT WAR-TORN COUNTRIES HAVE YOU VISITED?

OH, NONE OF THEM! WAR-TORN COUNTRIES AREN'T REALLY MY THING...

N.WILD 23.04.2007

SO WHY LIVE IN AFGHANISTAN, THEN?

WELL...THE WAR'S OVER IN AFGHANISTAN, ISN'T IT?

NOT EXACTLY...

IN MY ORGANIZATION, WE DON'T HIRE ANYONE UNDER THIRTY.

DESSERT

JUST THINK ABOUT IT! FOR OUR OWN SAFETY, WE NEVER LEAVE THE OFFICE OR THE GUESTHOUSE...

YOUNG PEOPLE ARE LIKE CAGED LIONS – THEY GO CRAZY.

THEY'RE GUARANTEED TO LOSE IT IN THREE MONTHS...

WELL, I'M ONLY GOING THERE FOR A TWO-MONTH JOB, ANYWAY...

THAT'S WHAT THEY ALL SAY, BUT THEY'RE STILL THERE TWO YEARS LATER, HANGING OUT IN THE SAME EXPAT RESTAURANTS...

...GOING TO THE SAME EXPAT PARTIES WITH THE SAME EXPATS.

ARE YOU AN ALCOHOLIC, MR. WILD?

IF NOT, YOU SOON WILL BE...

N.WILD 23.04.2007

12

I'LL BE WORKING ON A FASCINATING PROJECT IN KABUL...

PRODUCING COMICS TO EXPLAIN THE AFGHAN CONSTITUTION TO CHILDREN...

ANOTHER ILLUSTRATOR, TRISTAN BOUGON, IS THERE ALREADY, DOING THE STORYBOARDS.

THE MAIN CHARACTERS' NAMES ARE YASSIN AND KAKA RAOUF.

KAKA RAOUF'S SON WAS KILLED IN THE WAR, THEN HE ADOPTED YASSIN, WHO'D LOST HIS PARENTS...

EACH CHAPTER OF THEIR STORY EXPLORES ONE ARTICLE OF THE CONSTITUTION (PROHIBITION OF CHILD LABOR, GIRLS' RIGHT TO EDUCATION, ANTI-CORRUPTION LAWS, THE RIGHTS OF RETURNING AFGHAN REFUGEES...)

WELCOME TO KABUL

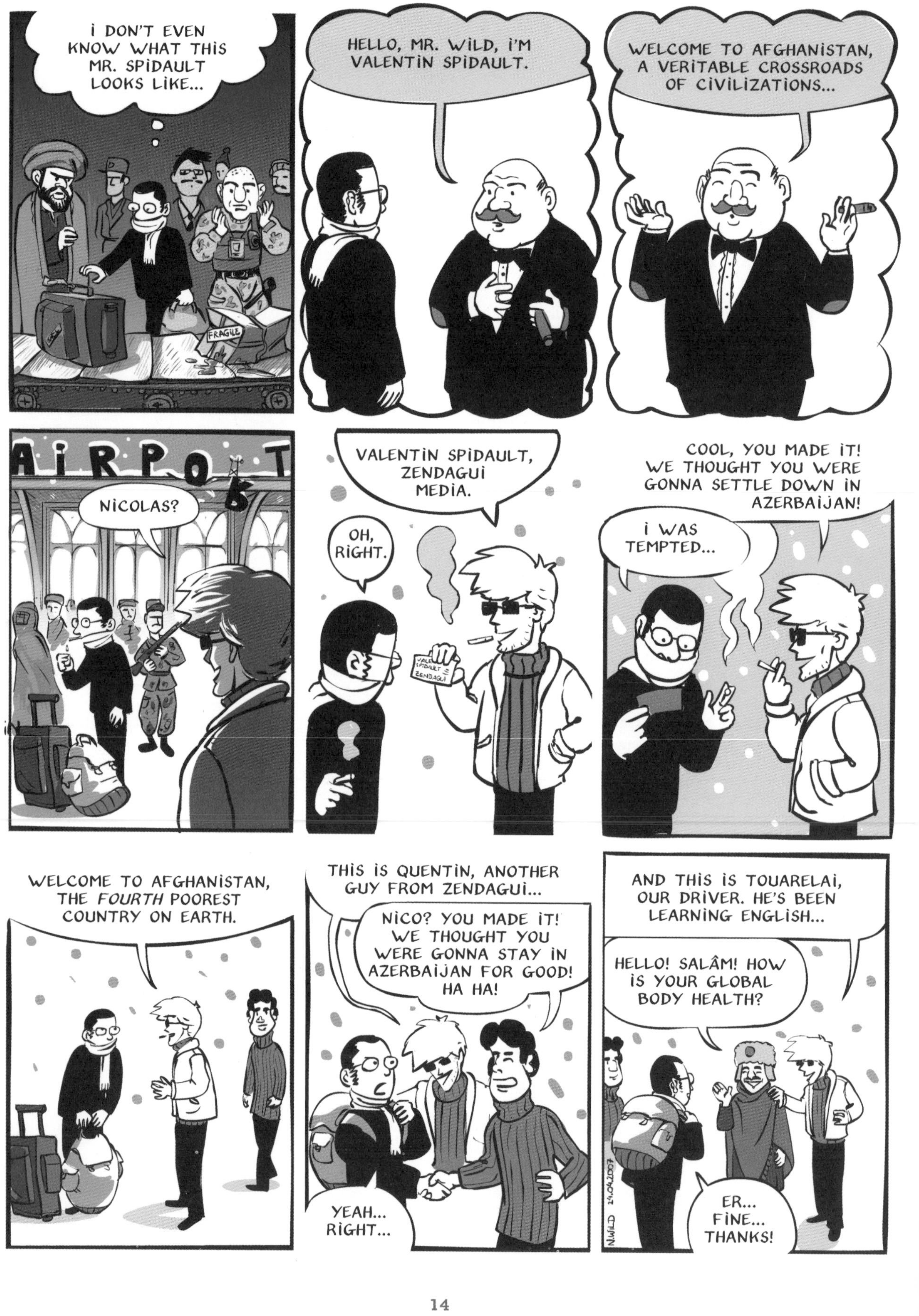

I DON'T EVEN KNOW WHAT THIS MR. SPIDAULT LOOKS LIKE...
FRAGILE
HELLO, MR. WILD, I'M VALENTIN SPIDAULT.
WELCOME TO AFGHANISTAN, A VERITABLE CROSSROADS OF CIVILIZATIONS...
NICOLAS?
VALENTIN SPIDAULT, ZENDAGUI MEDIA.
OH, RIGHT.
COOL, YOU MADE IT! WE THOUGHT YOU WERE GONNA SETTLE DOWN IN AZERBAIJAN!
I WAS TEMPTED...
WELCOME TO AFGHANISTAN, THE *FOURTH* POOREST COUNTRY ON EARTH.
THIS IS QUENTIN, ANOTHER GUY FROM ZENDAGUI...
NICO? YOU MADE IT! WE THOUGHT YOU WERE GONNA STAY IN AZERBAIJAN FOR GOOD! HA HA!
YEAH... RIGHT...
AND THIS IS TOUARELAI, OUR DRIVER. HE'S BEEN LEARNING ENGLISH...
HELLO! SALÂM! HOW IS YOUR GLOBAL BODY HEALTH?
ER... FINE... THANKS!

OK, NICO, OUR TOYOTA MINIBUS WILL TAKE US TO THE OFFICE. HOP IN!

HOLD UP, I'D LIKE TO SAY GOODBYE TO MY FRIENDS FROM BAKU...

THEY'RE ALREADY IN THE BUS. WE'LL DROP THEM OFF ON THE WAY!

YOUR NEW BOSS IS SUCH A NICE GUY!

?

SO, YOU HAD A NICE TRIP?

NOT REALLY, I--

BIDI BIDI

...

YEAH?

MR. SPIDAULT HAS AN AMAZING AMERICAN ACCENT...

HOW WAS THE TRIP?

YEAH?

IT WAS AWFUL, I--

SORRY, THIS CALL IS MORE IMPORTANT.

BIDI BIDI

YA?

YEAH!

FIRST IMPRESSIONS OF KABUL: THEY HAVE CELL PHONES...

15

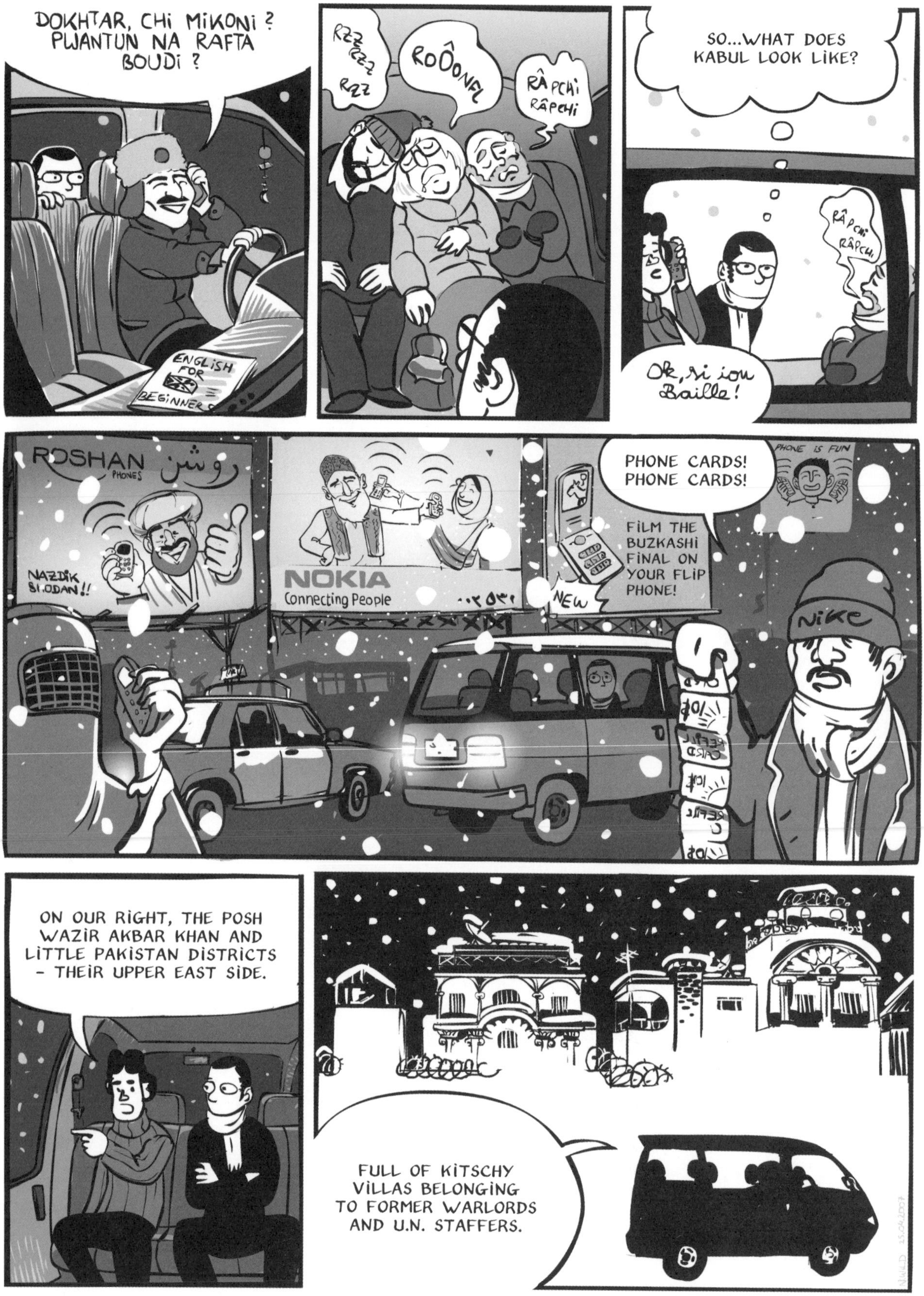
DOKHTAR, CHI MIKONI ? PWANTUN NA RAFTA BOUDI ?
ENGLISH FOR BEGINNERS
RZZ RZZZ RZZ
ROÔONFL
RÂPCHI RÂPCHI
SO...WHAT DOES KABUL LOOK LIKE?
RÂPCHI RÂPCHI
Ok, si iou Baille!
ROSHAN PHONES روشن
NAZDIK SHODAN!!
NOKIA
Connecting People
PHONE CARDS! PHONE CARDS!
PHONE IS FUN
FILM THE BUZKASHI FINAL ON YOUR FLIP PHONE!
NEW
NIKE
ON OUR RIGHT, THE POSH WAZIR AKBAR KHAN AND LITTLE PAKISTAN DISTRICTS - THEIR UPPER EAST SIDE.
FULL OF KITSCHY VILLAS BELONGING TO FORMER WARLORDS AND U.N. STAFFERS.

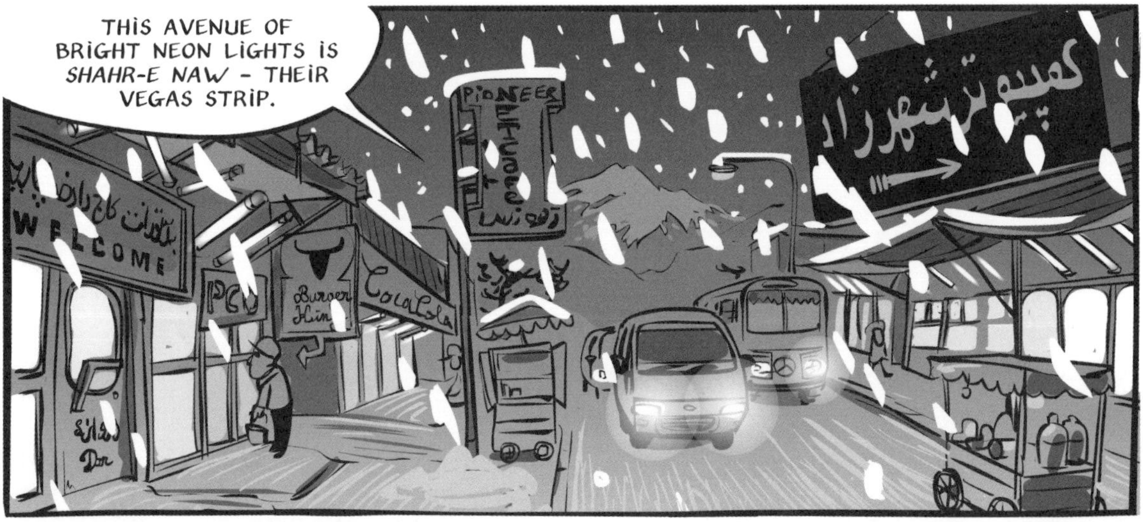
THIS AVENUE OF BRIGHT NEON LIGHTS IS *SHAHR-E NAW* - THEIR VEGAS STRIP.
WELCOME
PIONEER
Coca Cola

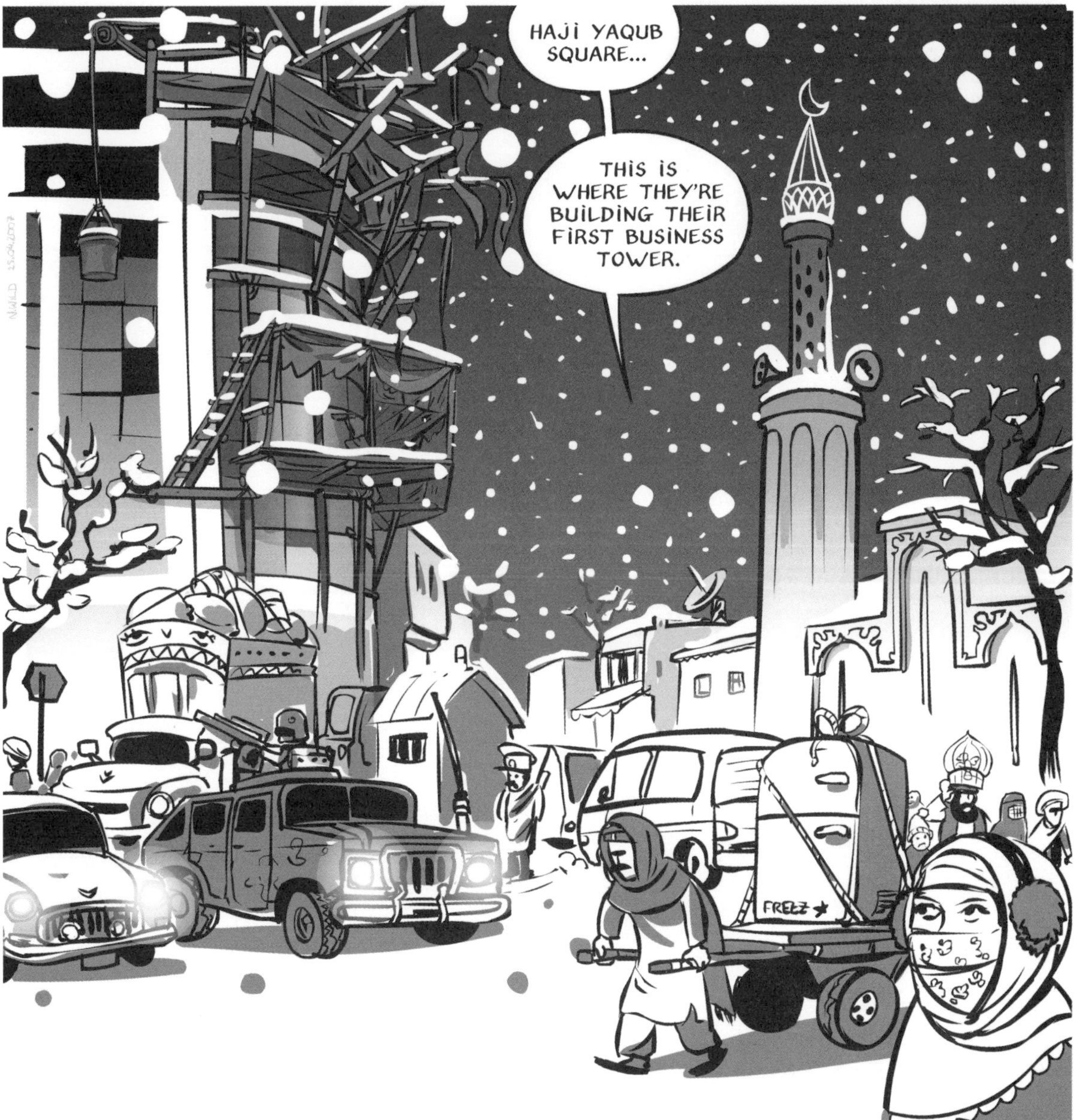
HAJI YAQUB SQUARE...
THIS IS WHERE THEY'RE BUILDING THEIR FIRST BUSINESS TOWER.
FREEZ

TA-DA! HERE'S OUR OFFICE!

IS THIS YOUR VERY OWN WALL STREET?

HABIBULLAH, THE OFFICE GUARD.

SALÂM ALEIKUM! KHOSH ÂMADI! SEHATET KHOUB AST! MÂNDA NA BÂSHI!

UH, WHAT IS HE SAYING?

"HELLO."

IT'S LATE, SO ALMOST EVERYONE'S LEFT ALREADY.

THAT TABLE IS THE GRAPHIC DESIGN DEPARTMENT. WE'LL CLEAR SOME SPACE FOR YOUR LAPTOP...

THAT'S QUENTIN'S DESK—THE LOGISTICS DEPARTMENT.

THE CIVIC EDUCATIONAL THEATER DEPARTMENT.

AND THAT DESK'S THE RADIO STUDIO.

SO WHICH DRAWER'S THE TOILET IN?

N.WILD 26.04.2007

TRISTAN, DON'T BE SUCH A GROUCH. SAY HI TO NICOLAS... HE'S COME FROM FAR AWAY TO DRAW STUFF WITH YOU!

YOU'RE GONNA HATE ME BY NEXT WEEK, MAN...

ORIGINALLY, WE HAD SEVEN WEEKS TO DRAW SIXTY PAGES OF COMICS...

...BUT THANKS TO YOUR LITTLE WEEK'S HOLIDAY IN AZERBAIJAN, WE NOW HAVE SIX...

DEADLINE'S JUST NOT DOABLE, UNLESS WE QUIT EATING AND SLEEPING...

...AND STITCH UP OUR BUTTHOLES TO CUT OUT TOILET TRIPS!

HERE'S THE AFGHAN CONSTITUTION THAT WE'LL BE WORKING ON.

MY GOD! THIS IS ONE *DENSE* DOCUMENT!

MY ADVICE: READ IT TONIGHT!

OK, TRISTAN, NICO... NOW THAT YOU'RE THE BEST OF BUDDIES, WANNA SWING BY MY PLACE FOR A FEW BEERS?

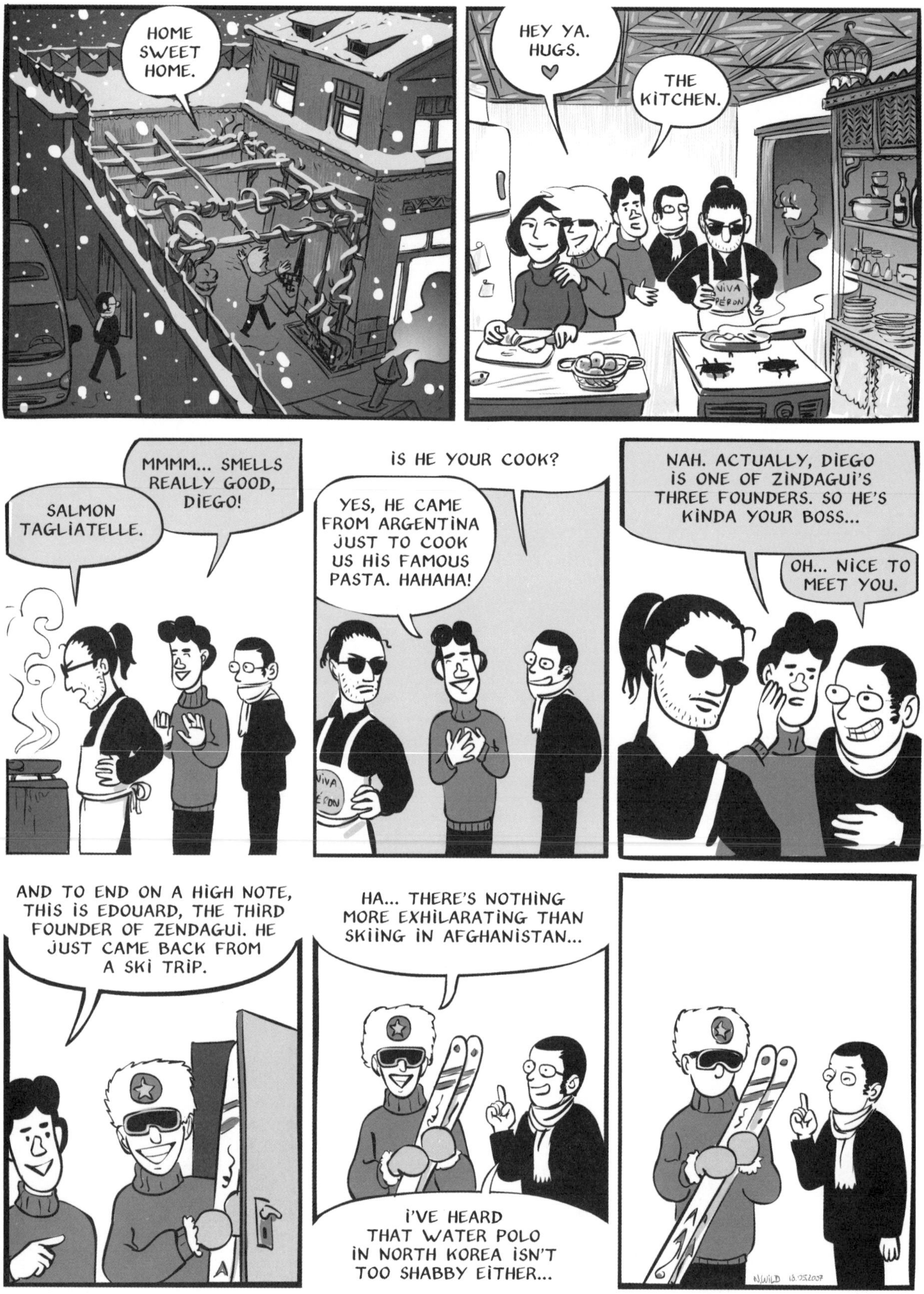
HOME SWEET HOME.
HEY YA. HUGS. ♥
THE KITCHEN.
VIVA PÉRON
SALMON TAGLIATELLE.
MMMM... SMELLS REALLY GOOD, DIEGO!
IS HE YOUR COOK?
YES, HE CAME FROM ARGENTINA JUST TO COOK US HIS FAMOUS PASTA. HAHAHA!
NAH. ACTUALLY, DIEGO IS ONE OF ZINDAGUI'S THREE FOUNDERS. SO HE'S KINDA YOUR BOSS...
OH... NICE TO MEET YOU.
AND TO END ON A HIGH NOTE, THIS IS EDOUARD, THE THIRD FOUNDER OF ZENDAGUI. HE JUST CAME BACK FROM A SKI TRIP.
HA... THERE'S NOTHING MORE EXHILARATING THAN SKIING IN AFGHANISTAN...
I'VE HEARD THAT WATER POLO IN NORTH KOREA ISN'T TOO SHABBY EITHER...
N.WILD 18.03.2007

WHO IS THIS GUY?

THE NEW ARTIST...

AH, NICOLAS! YOU MADE IT! THOUGHT YOU WERE GONNA SETTLE DOWN IN AZERBAIJAN!

I SHOULD HAVE...

HA HA!

HA HA!

HA HA!

TRISTAN, CAN I BUM A CIGGIE?

HA HA HA HA HA HA HA

HERE.

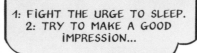

1: FIGHT THE URGE TO SLEEP. 2: TRY TO MAKE A GOOD IMPRESSION...

HA HA HA HA

CAN'T WAIT TO TASTE THAT CAVIAR YOU'VE BROUGHT FROM BAKU...

ER... ACTUALLY I DIDN'T BUY ANY, BECAUSE I'M BROKE...

HUH?

WHAT?

NOOO!

SHIT!

HA HA!

3: DIG MYSELF A LITTLE HOLE. 4: TURN INTO AN ANT. 5: HIDE IN THE HOLE...

HOOHOOHOO WAH HA HA!!!

21

THAT WAS THE BOSSES' GUESTHOUSE, IN HAJI YAQUB DISTRICT...

BUT WE LIVE WITH ZENDAGUI'S ENGLISH-SPEAKING EXPATS IN TAIMANI DISTRICT.

OUR GUESTHOUSE IS A REAL *PALACE*... THE PIPES BURST FROM THE COLD, SO WE'VE GOT NO WATER. YOUR BEDROOM CEILING LEAKS, AND WE ONLY GET ELECTRICITY EVERY OTHER DAY...

HERE IT IS!

HM, SO WHAT ARCHITECTURAL STYLE IS THIS?

DUNNO. SOVIET SWISS CHALET?

THIS IS YOUR ROOM.

IT HITS -15° CELSIUS AT NIGHT. GET THE GUARD TO LIGHT YOUR BOKHÂRI...

GOODNIGHT!

VLAM

OK... THE AFGHAN CONSTITUTION...

"CHAPTER ONE..."

"AFGHANISTAN IS AN ISLAMIC REPUBLIC..."

ZZZ

HELLO, I'M THE AFGHAN CONSTITUTION.

PERHAPS YOU'VE ALREADY SEEN ME IN THE EXCELLENT YASSIN & KAKA RAOUF COMICS...

TODAY, I'M A DEMOCRATIC CONSTITUTION THAT RESPECTS THE QUR'ĀN AND HUMAN RIGHTS.

BUT THAT HASN'T ALWAYS BEEN THE CASE...

NEXT SLIDE!

UNTIL 1963, I WAS THE CONSTITUTION OF AN AUTHORITARIAN MONARCHY. IN 1964, KING ZAHIR SHAH DISMISSED THE THEN PRIME MINISTER, HIS COUSIN DAOUD.

ZAHIR SHAH REWROTE ME...

THAT TICKLES!

...THUS PAVING THE WAY FOR DEMOCRACY. I BECAME THE CONSTITUTION OF A PARLIAMENTARY MONARCHY.

IRONICALLY, THAT VERY DEMOCRACY FOSTERED THE CREATION OF ANTI-DEMOCRATIC PARTIES...

ON THE ONE HAND, RELIGIOUS EXTREMIST PARTIES LIKE THE ONE LED BY GULBUDDIN HEKMATYAR...

AND ON THE OTHER, THE COMMUNIST PARTY, SPLIT INTO TWO RIVAL FACTIONS...

PARCHAM, LED BY KARMAL...

AND KHALQ, LED BY TARAKI AND AMIN.

PARLIAMENTARY CRISES AND FAMINE DESTABILIZED THE KINGDOM. IN 1973, DAOUD ORGANIZED A COUP D'ÉTAT WITH THE ARMY'S SUPPORT...

REVENGE.

SO ENDS THE REIGN OF ZAHIR SHAH THE DESPOT!

TU QUOQUE, FILI MI!

A CONNOISSEUR OF LATIN PHRASES, THE KING EXILED HIMSELF TO ROME.

DAOUD REWROTE ME...

HEE HEE!

NOW I'M THE CONSTITUTION OF THE REPUBLIC OF AFGHANISTAN...

DAOUD'S COMMUNIST ALLIES HAD A STRONG FOOTHOLD IN THE MINISTRIES AND THE ARMY.

EVERY YEAR, THEY GAINED POWER AND POPULARITY, WHICH WORRIED DAOUD...

GRIPPED BY PARANOIA, HE FEARED A COUP D'ÉTAT. ON 25 APRIL, 1978, HE IMPRISONED KARMAL AND TARAKI.

AMIN WAS PLACED UNDER HOUSE ARREST, BUT THE POLICE GUARDING HIM WERE DEVOTED SUPPORTERS WHO ALLOWED HIM CONTACT WITH THE OUTSIDE WORLD.

TEA?

MOST OFFICERS HAD BEEN TRAINED IN MOSCOW AND WERE PRO-COMMUNIST. AMIN ORDERED THEM TO SEIZE THE PRESIDENTIAL PALACE...

SO ENDS THE REIGN OF DAOUD THE TYRANT!

DAOUD REFUSED TO SURRENDER. HE AND HIS FAMILY WERE UNCEREMONIOUSLY EXECUTED.

I WAS RETOOLED ONCE AGAIN...

SO, I'LL BE THE PRESIDENT!

OK, BUT I'LL BE VICE-PRESIDENT AND PRIME MINISTER!

OH, CAN I BE VICE-PREMIER AND FOREIGN MINISTER THEN?

FROM LEFT TO RIGHT:

I BECAME THE CONSTITUTION OF THE "DEMOCRATIC REPUBLIC OF AFGHANISTAN." EVVIVA IL COMUNISMO E LA LIBERTÀ!

THE COMMUNISTS? HUH! IF ONLY YOU KNEW WHAT ATROCITIES THEY COMMITTED IN MY NAME!

BANNING MUSLIM WORSHIP, FOR INSTANCE! IMAGINE THE BEWILDERMENT OF THE AFGHAN PEOPLE, WHOSE RELIGION IS THE HEART OF SOCIETY AND LIFE ITSELF...

ALL THOSE OPPOSING THE REGIME WERE SENT TO CONCENTRATION CAMPS. SAYED ABDULLAH, CHIEF WARDEN OF PUL-E-CHARKHI PRISON, DECLARED:

A MILLION AFGHANS ARE ALL THAT SHOULD STAY ALIVE! THAT'S ENOUGH TO BUILD COMMUNISM!

REBELLION WAS BREWING NATIONWIDE... SOLDIERS DESERTED TO JOIN THE UNDERGROUND...

THE FINAL STRUGGLE WILL NOT GET PAST US!

IN MARCH 1979, PROTESTS BROKE OUT IN HERAT.

KARMAL AND TARAKI WERE OUT OF THEIR DEPTH...

TARAKI MET BREZHNEV IN MOSCOW. THEY CONCOCTED A PLAN TO REGAIN THE AFGHAN PEOPLE'S TRUST – A STALINIST SHOW TRIAL, WHERE AMIN WOULD BE HELD SOLELY RESPONSIBLE FOR THE AFGHAN COMMUNIST PARTY'S MISTAKES.

HA HA!

HEE HEE!

WHEN TARAKI RETURNED, AMIN DISCOVERED THE PLOT AND HAD HIM KILLED.

REVOLUTION-STEALER!

AMIN BECAME PRESIDENT...

...BUT WAS STILL UNABLE TO RESTORE ORDER IN THE COUNTRY. RELUCTANTLY, HE ASKED FOR MOSCOW'S HELP...

BREJNEV.

BREZHNEV SENT IN SEVERAL RED ARMY BATTALIONS TO REINFORCE THE AFGHAN ARMY, WHICH WAS STILL FIGHTING THE INSURGENTS.

THE FIRST RUSSIAN OFFICERS TO ARRIVE IN KABUL ALSO HAD A SECRET MISSION: TO ASSASSINATE AMIN. BREZHNEV NEVER FORGAVE HIM FOR TARAKI'S MURDER.

SO IT WAS KARMAL'S TURN TO BE PRESIDENT OF WHAT WAS FAST BECOMING THE MOST UNGOVERNABLE COUNTRY ON EARTH.

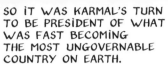

AS THE DAYS WORE ON, RUSSIA'S SUPPORT WAS SO PLENTIFUL THAT IT BECAME MORE LIKE AN INVASION.

WAR BROKE OUT...

AFGHANISTAN BECAME THE THEATER OF ONE OF THE LAST AND CRUELEST EPISODES OF THE COLD WAR.

THE RED ARMY SEEMED TO HAVE TAKEN SAYED ABDULLAH'S PROPHETIC WORDS TO HEART: "A MILLION AFGHANS ARE ALL THAT SHOULD STAY ALIVE..."

THE INTERNATIONAL COMMUNITY TURNED A BLIND EYE AS THE POPULATION WAS MASSACRED.

IN 1985, MILLIONS OF AFGHANS FLED THE COUNTRY IN ONE OF THE LARGEST EXODUSES OF THE TWENTIETH CENTURY...

...WHILE THOSE WHO STAYED BEHIND PUT UP A HEROIC, RELENTLESS FIGHT AGAINST THE RUSSIANS.

GOD, I'M FREEZING.

THAT MUST BE THE "BOKHÂRI"...

NEED TO FIND SOME PAPER QUICK AND GET THE FIRE GOING.

GODDAMMIT... NEVER TRAVEL WITHOUT A DECENT SUPPLY OF NEWSPAPER...

THE AFGHAN CONSTITUTION

THE AFGHAN CONSTITUTION

THE AFGHAN CONSTITUTION

THE AFGHAN CONSTITUTION

ONE HOUR AND ONE BURNT CONSTITUTION LATER...

THE FIRE WON'T LIGHT! BOOHOO!!!

BOKHÂRI RÂ JOR KONOM?

ARE YOU THE GUARD? DO YOU SPEAK ENGLISH?

MA CHAWDIKÂR HASTAM.

BLOUP

BLOUP

SCRATCH

BROUF

TASHAKOR.

QABELESH NEST.

IN A COUNTRY WITH AN 80% ILLITERACY RATE, I GUESS NEWSPAPER MUST BE RARER THAN GASOLINE...

GOD, I'M SWELTERING!

29

BOULET, DID YOU MAKE COFFEE?

♫ ALLAH ALLAHU AKBAR ♫

FLOP FLOP
FLOP FLOP FLOP
FLOP FLOP
FLOP

GOOOOOOD MORNING, AFGHANISTAN!!!

WHY DID I OPEN THE FRIDGE?

PANCAKE?

AAH!

PANCAKE! I MAKE IT SPECIAL FOR YOU, SIR! HA HA HA!

HA HA HA

SPECIAL FOR YOU...

GOOOOD PANCAKE I MAKE.

THAT'S KÂKÂR, OUR COOK.

MAHBUBA, OUR CLEANING LADY.

FROT FROT

EXPAT LIFE HERE IS A MIXED BAG.

PANCAKE IS READY, SIR.

THE CAR LEAVES AT 8:45, SO YOU'VE GOT 10 MINUTES TO EAT YOUR PANCAKE...

HELLO!

I'M NICOLAS, THE NEW ILLUSTRATOR...

NICE TO MEET YOU! I'M AKRAM, IN CHARGE OF RESEARCH AT ZENDAGUI.

OH? WHAT ARE YOU SEARCHING FOR?

I'LL KNOW WHEN I FIND IT.

I MEANT, WHAT ARE YOU RESEARCHING?

I'M NOT AUTHORIZED TO SHARE THAT INFORMATION.

SERIOUSLY? YOU'RE A SPY? ARE YOU AFTER OSAMA BIN LADEN?

HA HA!

SLURP

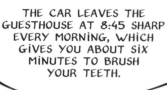

THE CAR LEAVES THE GUESTHOUSE AT 8:45 SHARP EVERY MORNING, WHICH GIVES YOU ABOUT SIX MINUTES TO BRUSH YOUR TEETH.

SIX MINUTES LATER...

OPERATION "ENDURING BOREDOM" INITIATED.

IT WOULD BE A BIT BORING TO INTRODUCE ALL OF ZENDAGUI'S EMPLOYEES...

...AND MENTION ALL OF ITS PROJECTS...

SALÂM ALEIKUM! KHOSH ÂMADI! BÂ SEHAT KHUB ASTI! MÂNDA NA BÂSHI!

LIKEWISE.

...BUT I'M GOING TO DO IT ANYWAY, ON ONE PAGE (I LIKE A CHALLENGE).

JORDAN, AUSTRALIAN, MANAGES THE NJTP.*

*NOVICE JOURNALISM TRAINING PROGRAM, AIMED AT IMPROVING HOW JOURNALISM IS TAUGHT AT EIGHT OF THE COUNTRY'S UNIVERSITIES.

HE IS ASSISTED BY KELLY, ALSO FROM AUSTRALIA, AND SUSHIL, AN INDIAN GUY WHO STUDIED IN LONDON.

AZIZ IS ZENDAGUI'S THEATER SPECIALIST. A PROLIFIC AUTHOR, HIS SOCIAL AND CIVIC PLAYS ARE STAGED BY A DOZEN TROUPES ACROSS THE COUNTRY.

LAST YEAR'S PLAY WAS ABOUT THE PRESIDENTIAL ELECTIONS, AND HE IS CURRENTLY WORKING ON ONE ABOUT PARLIAMENTARY ELECTIONS.

LIMA AND IBRAHIM MANAGE THE FINANCES AND ACCOUNTS. RAMIN TAKES CARE OF THE RADIO STUDIO.

THEN THERE'S THE MYSTERIOUS AKRAM, ORIGINALLY FROM BANGLADESH, WHO IS HELPED IN HIS "RESEARCH" BY TWO AFGHANS: AHMED AND DR. CHARCHESHM.

4 GUARDS, 3 DRIVERS, 2 CLEANING LADIES AND 2 COOKS TO PROTECT, CHAUFFEUR, CLEAN AND FEED EVERYBODY.

ZENDAGUI'S THREE FOUNDERS ARE IN CHARGE OF EVERYONE.
THREE BOSSES WITH THREE DIFFERENT STYLES...

EDOUARD IS FRENCH...

ALL GRAPHIC DESIGNERS WILL GET A RAISE...

SERIOUSLY?!

...IN WORKING HOURS!

I HATE HIM.

VALENTIN IS ALSO FRENCH...

SO, MY CHICKADEES! ONE DAY YOU'LL HAVE TO STOP DRAWING PICTURES AND GET PROPER JOBS! HA HA!

I LOVE MY GRAPHIC DESIGNERS...

...THEY'RE BRIGHT-EYED...

...AND BUSHY-TAILED!

AND HOW ARE THINGS WITH HARUN? I HIRED HIM FOR HIS LOOKS...

US GOOD-LOOKING GUYS HAVE TO STICK TOGETHER.

AND DIEGO, AN EXTREME ADVENTURER FROM ARGENTINA.

HE'S WORKED IN KOSOVO, EAST TIMOR, AND OTHER WAR-TORN COUNTRIES...

VLING

¡PUTA!

NESCAFÉ IS DISGUSTING!

AND THEN THERE'S TRISTAN, HARUN AND MYSELF: THE GRAPHIC DESIGN AND ART TEAM.

DUE TO THE DEADLINE, WE WON'T HAVE TIME TO LEAVE THE OFFICE TO MAKE PREPARATORY SKETCHES...

DAMN.

THAT'S WHY EDOUARD HAS KINDLY LENT US HIS EXTERNAL HARD DRIVE. IT'S CRAMMED WITH PHOTOS OF AFGHANISTAN.

WE CAN USE THEM AS A BASIS FOR THE BACKGROUNDS AND CHARACTERS IN THE COMIC.

BEEP

EDOUARD IN BAMIYAN...

EDOUARD SKIING IN SALANG...

EDOUARD IN MAZAR-E SHARIF FOR NEW YEAR'S...

EDOUARD AT THE HILTON DUBAI...

EDOUARD RIDING A YAK IN WARDAK PROVINCE...

I BET SENDING THIS HARD DRIVE TO FRANCE WOULD'VE COST LESS THAN FLYING US OUT TO KABUL.

DUBAI LOOKS COOL!

YOU BETCHA!

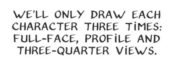

Panel 1: TO SAVE TIME, WE'LL DRAW STRAIGHT ONTO THE COMPUTER USING A GRAPHICS TABLET.

OH?

Panel 2: WE'LL ONLY DRAW EACH CHARACTER THREE TIMES: FULL-FACE, PROFILE AND THREE-QUARTER VIEWS.

COOL.

Panel 3: THEN WE CAN COPY/PASTE THEM AS MUCH AS WE LIKE.

YEAH?

Panel 4: AREN'T YOU AFRAID IT'LL BE OBVIOUSLY FAKE?

NAH.

Panel 5: WE'LL BE CLEVER, BY FLIPPING THE IMAGE HORIZONTALLY, FOR EXAMPLE.

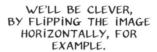

WHOA.

Panel 6: THAT'S SMART.

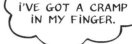

Panel 7: OR WE CAN THROW IN A DETAIL FROM TIME TO TIME, TO COVER OUR TRACKS.

WILD!

Panel 8: LIKE HATS, FOR EXAMPLE...

OH?

Panel 9: I'VE GOT A CRAMP IN MY FINGER.

ZENDAGUI OFFERS ITS EXPATS DARI LESSONS (DARI IS THE PERSIAN SPOKEN IN AFGHANISTAN, AND IS SIMILAR TO THE FARSI SPOKEN IN IRAN).

FOR OUR FIFTH DARI LESSON, WE WILL TAKE A CLOSER LOOK AT POLITE FORMS.

OH NO...

YAK YAHÀN TACHAKOR = UN MERCI GROS COMME UNE PLANÈTE

THIS SUCKS.

CAN'T WE LEARN SOME CURSE WORDS INSTEAD?

CU-CURSE WORDS? BUT I... I...

YEAH! IF WE'RE GONNA BE STAYING HERE A WHILE, THEY'LL COME IN HANDY...

PLEASE! WE ARE A VERY POLITE PEOPLE... THERE ARE NO SUCH WORDS IN DARI...

YOU'RE TRYING TO TELL US THAT IN 23 YEARS OF WAR, NOT ONE AFGHAN WAS EVER TEMPTED TO INSULT ANYBODY?

EXCUSE ME SIR, WOULD YOU KINDLY ALLOW ME TO BURN YOUR HOUSE DOWN AND RAPE YOUR WIFE?

HEE HEE

WHY, OF COURSE, DEAR FRIEND! BE MY GUEST!

FINE. THEN I'D LIKE TO KNOW HOW TO TELL A GIRL SHE'S PRETTY...

ALL RIGHT THEN... INSULTS...

KHAR ASTI! = YOU ARE A DONKEY!

KHAR

ALTHOUGH THE JOB IS INTERESTING, IT'S TAKING UP ALL OUR TIME, WEEKENDS AND EVENINGS INCLUDED.

GOD'S PUNISHING ME FOR ALL THE TIMES I DIDN'T WORK.

YOU KNOW WHERE VAL, EDOUARD AND THE OTHERS ARE RIGHT NOW?

UH...

HAVING DRINKS AT LA *JOIE DE VIVRE*, THE FRENCH RESTAURANT.

THERE'S A FRENCH RESTAURANT IN KABUL?!

YES. PATHETIC, ISN'T IT? FOR ME, COMING TO AFGHANISTAN WAS ALL ABOUT A SIMPLER LIFE, IMMERSING MYSELF IN ANOTHER CULTURE.

DON'T YOU AGREE?

WHAT'S THE POINT OF COMING TO KABUL JUST TO EAT FOIE GRAS AND GET DRUNK ON COGNAC EVERY NIGHT? HONESTLY!

ALL THE FRENCH OUT HERE ARE BOBOS — BOURGEOIS BOHEMIANS. THEY MISS HIGH SOCIETY SO MUCH THAT THEY'VE RECREATED A CHUNK OF PARIS IN CENTRAL KABUL: LA *JOIE DE VIVRE*. IT'S A *DISGRACE!*

WELL, WE'LL NEVER GO THERE. WE'RE MOMOS.

WE'RE WHAT?

MOMOS— MONEYLESS MORONS...

HA HA HA!

HA HA!

THIS EVENING, THE SHIITES OF KABUL ARE MARKING ASHURA, TO COMMEMORATE THE DEATH OF THE PROPHET'S GRANDSON, ALI.

ALI... O ALI... ALI... O

ALI... ALI... O ALI... ALI...

ALI... O ALI... ALI... O

ALI... ALI... O ALI... ALI...

IN A SHOW OF SYMPATHY FOR THE PROPHET'S SUFFERING, THE FAITHFUL FLOG THEMSELVES THROUGHOUT THE CEREMONY WHILE MULLAHS RECITE POETRY AND SACRED TEXTS IN PRAISE OF ALI.

THEORETICALLY, WE AREN'T ALLOWED TO ATTEND THIS CEREMONY...

I PROMISED THE MULLAH WHO LET US IN THAT WE'D BE REALLY DISCREET.

RELAX, VAL...

FLASH

CLIK

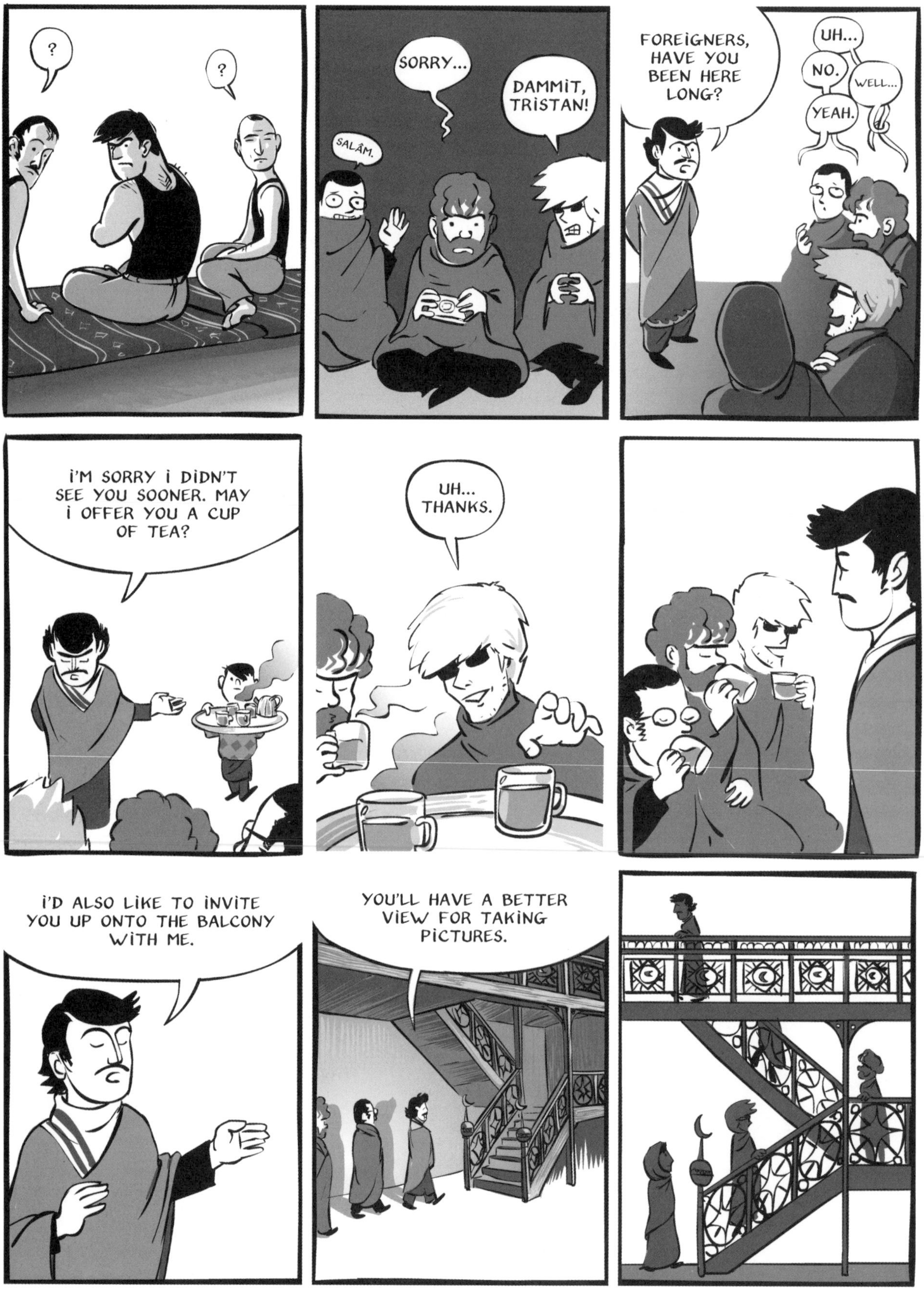
?
?
SALÂM.
SORRY...
DAMMIT, TRISTAN!
FOREIGNERS, HAVE YOU BEEN HERE LONG?
UH...
NO.
WELL...
YEAH.
I'M SORRY I DIDN'T SEE YOU SOONER. MAY I OFFER YOU A CUP OF TEA?
UH... THANKS.
I'D ALSO LIKE TO INVITE YOU UP ONTO THE BALCONY WITH ME.
YOU'LL HAVE A BETTER VIEW FOR TAKING PICTURES.

HEY! LOOK THERE! THAT MULLAH'S SMOKING!

IF THE MULLAH HIMSELF CAN SMOKE...

THIS MUST BE A SMOKING MOSQUE...

EXCUSE ME, FOREIGNER, HOW DO CHRISTIANS HONOR THE DEATH OF CHRIST?

?

WELL...WE ALL WEAR CROWNS OF THORNS ON OUR HEADS...

AND WE WANDER THE STREETS ALL DAY, CARRYING HUGE WOODEN CROSSES...

WOOF

IN THE EVENING, PRIESTS HAMMER RUSTY NAILS INTO OUR HANDS AND FEET.

HALLELUJAH!

AND WE SING TILL DAWN OF THE JOY OF SUFFERING TOGETHER WITH CHRIST.

NAH, I'M JUST KIDDING. WE CHRISTIANS HAVE TURNED INTO REAL WIMPS OVER THE YEARS. WE CAN'T COPE WITH PHYSICAL TORTURE...

WE BARELY COMMEMORATE THE DEATH OF CHRIST, BUT WE DO MARK HIS RESURRECTION THREE DAYS LATER. IT'S CALLED EASTER!

WE HIDE CHOCOLATE EGGS AND RABBITS IN THE GARDEN FOR CHILDREN TO FIND...

THEN THERE'S A MEAL, AND PARENTS OPEN UP A FEW BOTTLES OF GOOD WINE TO GO WITH EXPENSIVE, REFINED DISHES LIKE FOIE GRAS.

PLOP

HAPPY EASTER!

BOOK ONE OF THE ADVENTURES OF YASSIN & KAKA RAOUF COVERS THE PROHIBITION OF CHILD LABOR...

BUT I STILL BUY MY SMOKES FROM A 5-YEAR-OLD KID EVERY MORNING.

POOR LITTLE THING... SHE'D BE MUCH BETTER OFF AT SCHOOL...

40 AFGHANIS.

?

BUT THEY WERE 36 YESTERDAY...

QIMAT AST!*

QIMATY AST!**

*THAT'S EXPENSIVE!
**THAT'S INFLATION!

AGAR ZENDAGI DAR KABOL QIMAT AST, BORD BYÂDAR DAR BADAKHSHÂN!*

*IF LIFE IN KABUL IS TOO EXPENSIVE FOR YOU, JUST MOVE TO BADAKHSHÂN!

PAYSA BYÂR, KHÂRIJI!

HA HA HA!

HA HA HA!

DAMN BRATS...

NW 26.04.2007

CIGARETTES!

THANKS. EDOUARD WANTS TO SEE YOU IN HIS OFFICE.

EDOUARD?

SIT DOWN.

NICO, YOU'VE BEEN WITH US FOR NEARLY A MONTH...

UH, YEAH.

FROM NOW ON, I'D LIKE TO SEE YOU MORE ENGAGED IN THE DECISION-MAKING PROCESS AT ZENDAGUI.

UH... OKAY.

CLAP

I CAN SENSE YOU'RE A MAN OF IDEAS. I SEE GREAT QUALITIES IN YOU JUST *WAITING* TO BE REVEALED...

FOR SURE.

WE'RE THROWING A PARTY AT OUR GUESTHOUSE ON THURSDAY NIGHT. THE THEME IS "THE RETURN OF THE SUN." COME UP WITH SOME IDEAS FOR THE DECORATIONS.

A PARTY?

A PARTY!

THE SUN, THE BEACH, WOMEN...

FOR THE RETURN OF THE SUN?

WELL... YOU COULD FILL A ROOM WITH YELLOW BALLOONS...

THEN PAINT BIG SUNFLOWERS ALL OVER THE CEILING...

AND YOU COULD PROJECT BAYWATCH EPISODES ONTO A GIANT SCREEN!

THERE YOU GO...

FANTASTIC! BRILLIANT! I KNEW YOU WERE THE RIGHT MAN FOR THE JOB.

HOW MUCH TIME AND MONEY DO YOU NEED TO GET IT ALL READY?

WHAT?

I HAVEN'T GOT THE TIME TO DEAL WITH THAT! WE'VE GOT AN INCREDIBLE AMOUNT OF WORK TO DO...

OH... I'M DISAPPOINTED. I THOUGHT YOU WANTED TO GET MORE ENGAGED AT ZENDAGUI.

BUT I...

THAT'S NOT THE PROBLEM. I'VE GOT TO FINISH THE BOOK...

FORGET IT, NICOLAS. I'LL ASK SOMEBODY ELSE...

I'M *TERRIBLY* DISAPPOINTED!

45

WHERE WERE YOU?

OUT BUYING BALLOONS...

BALLOONS?

YES, BALLOONS. YELLOW ONES.

YELLOW... BALLOONS.

WE'RE RUNNING OUT OF TIME, THE PRINTER'S COMING IN AN HOUR, SO YOU THINK: "HEY, WHY DON'T I GO BUY MYSELF SOME BALLOONS?"

YOU GOT ME! I HAD A CRAVING FOR BALLOONS. JUST COULDN'T RESIST BUYING SOME. IT HAPPENS SOMETIMES, YOU KNOW?

THANKS FOR THE BALLOONS, NICO. HERE'S A PARTY INVITE FOR YOU!

BRING YOUR FRIENDS, IF YOU HAVE ANY...

AND HERE I WAS THINKING YOU WERE DIFFERENT, BUT YOU'RE *JUST* LIKE THEM.

YOU SNAKE!

YEAH, EXACTLY. I CAME TO KABUL TO PARTY HARD AND LIVE IT UP! I'M GIVING EDOUARD BALLOONS SO THAT HE'LL LIKE ME!

YOU'VE EXPOSED MY TRUE PERSONALITY. WELL DONE!

OK, OK... TAKE IT EASY. YOU'RE GETTING A LITTLE UPTIGHT THERE. HOW ABOUT SOME TEA?

ALRIGHT. I'LL JUST WHIP UP A DRAWING OF AFGHAN PARLIAMENT MEMBERS BEFORE THE PRINTER GETS HERE.

UH, ANY IDEA WHAT THE AFGHAN PARLIAMENT LOOKS LIKE?

ASK RAMIN TO HELP YOU DIG UP SOME INFO...

RAMIN, COULD YOU HELP ME DIG UP SOME INFO ON THE AFGHAN PARLIAMENT?

AIN'T NONE...

YES, THAT'S THE PROBLEM. I NEED TO FIND SOME.

NO, I MEAN AFGHANISTAN HAS NO PARLIAMENT.

...

ER...EDOUARD? VAL?

YEAH?

I'VE GOT AN HOUR TO DRAW THE AFGHAN PARLIAMENT, BUT I JUST FOUND OUT THERE ISN'T ONE...

SURE, IT HASN'T BEEN ELECTED YET. THE ELECTION DATE'S SET FOR SEPTEMBER 18TH.

OH, RIGHT. THEN WHAT SHOULD I DRAW FOR NOW?

JUST MAKE IT SYMBOLIC WITH RESPECT TO THE ETHNIC MAKEUP: 45% PASHTUNS, 36% TAJIKS, 12% UZBEKS AND 14% HAZARAS. PLUS A FEW NURISTANIS, OF COURSE. DRAW SOME WEARING SHALWAR KAMEEZ WITH TURBANS, PATUS OR PAKOLS, AND OTHERS WEARING THREE-PIECE SUITS. MAKE 25% OF THE 300 MEMBERS WOMEN.

OK, THANKS.

WHO WAS THAT? NICOLAS OR TRISTAN? I ALWAYS GET THEM MIXED UP...

DON'T WORRY, DIEGO, SOON THERE WILL ONLY BE ONE...

ER... VAL?

NOW WHAT?

SORRY FOR ALL THE DUMB QUESTIONS, BUT COULD YOU GIVE ME AN IDEA OF WHAT PASHTUNS, TAJIKS, UZBEKS, HAZARAS, NURISTANIS, SHALWAR KAMEEZ, PATUS, PAKOLS AND WOMEN LOOK LIKE?

ASK RAMIN TO HELP YOU DIG UP SOME IMAGES...

YEAH. OK. THANKS.

SOMEDAY WE SHOULD TELL HIM THIS IS AFGHANISTAN. I DON'T THINK HE GETS IT.

YOUNGSTER'S IN FOR A SHOCK.

HA HA!

WHAT DID YOU PUT IN THE AD, VAL? "SEEKS COMIC ARTIST" OR "SEEKS AUTISTIC COMIC"?

HO HO!

HEE HEE!

THURSDAY, MARCH 17TH, 2005. A KABUL STREET...

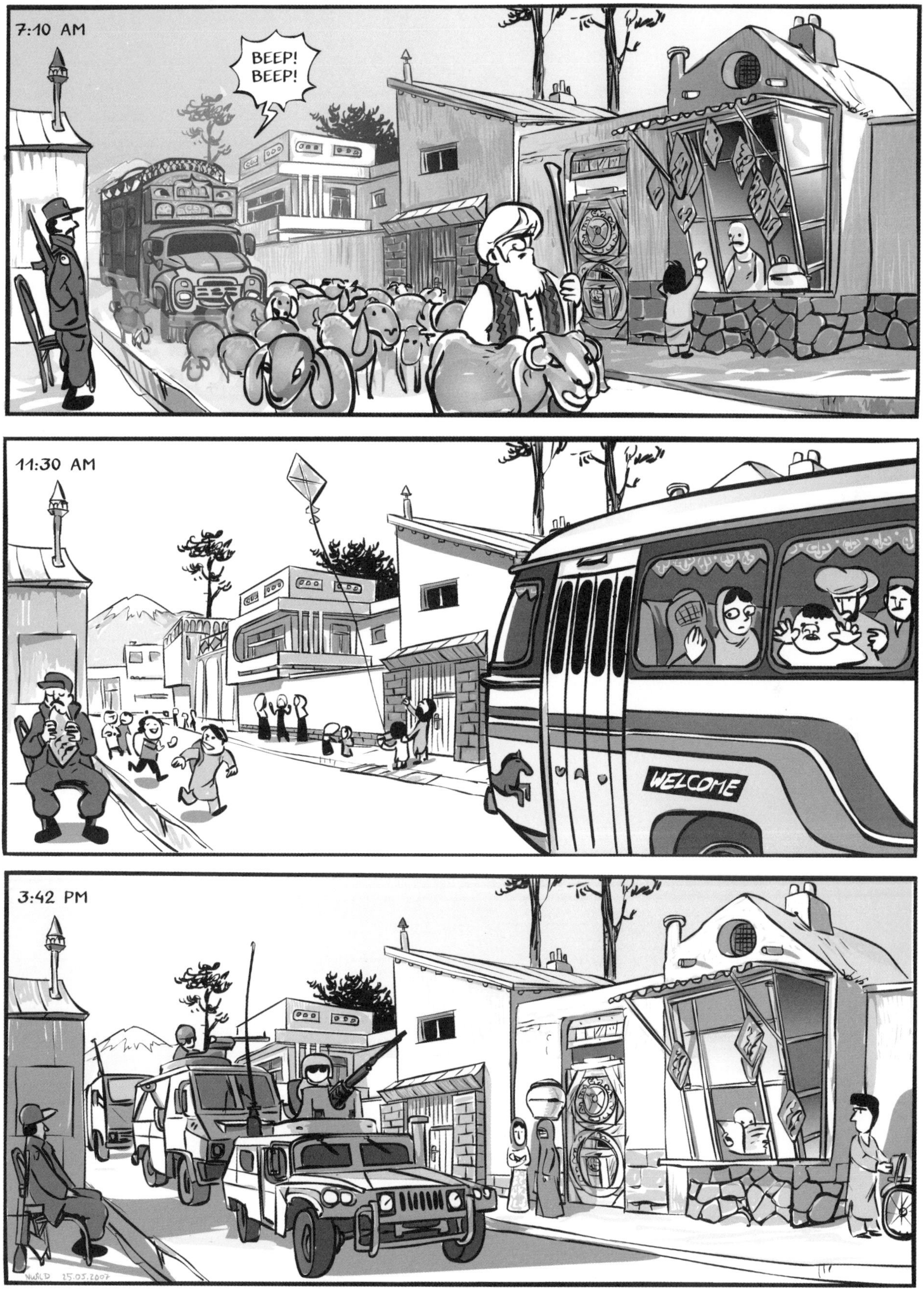
7:10 AM
BEEP! BEEP!
11:30 AM
WELCOME
3:42 PM

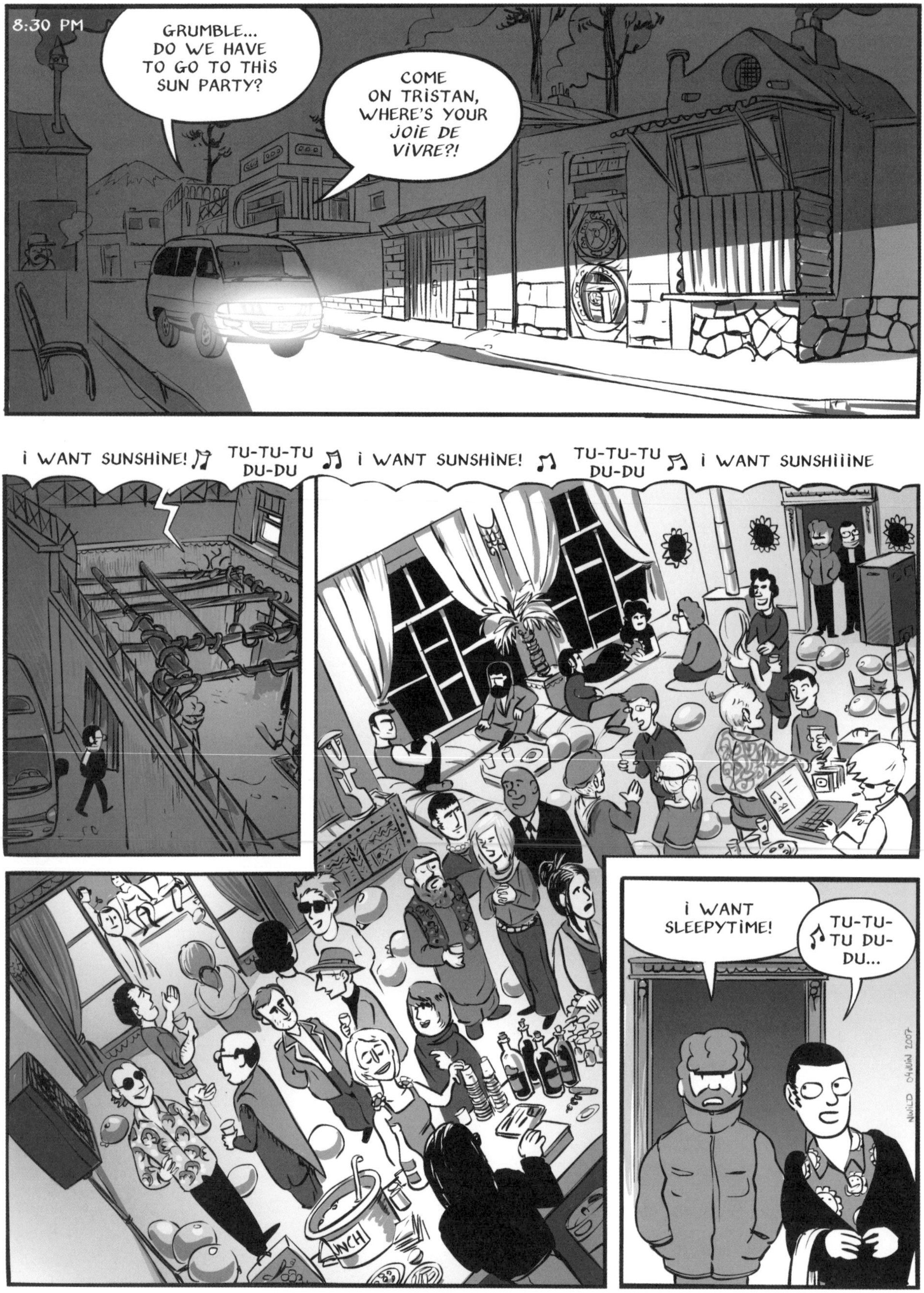
8:30 PM
GRUMBLE... DO WE HAVE TO GO TO THIS SUN PARTY?
COME ON TRISTAN, WHERE'S YOUR JOIE DE VIVRE?!
I WANT SUNSHINE!
TU-TU-TU DU-DU
I WANT SUNSHINE!
TU-TU-TU DU-DU
I WANT SUNSHIIINE
I WANT SLEEPYTIME!
TU-TU-TU DU-DU...

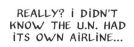

*FAMOUS FRENCH POP-ROCK BAND.

ACCORDING TO THE PERSIAN CALENDAR, THIS IS THE YEAR 1483.

OH! NOW I UNDERSTAND WHY THE INTERNET DOESN'T EVER WORK...

HA HA!

HI!

CAN YOU GUYS PLEASE TELL ME WHERE AKRAM IS?

SHIT! AMERICAN SOLDIERS!

WHERE IS AKRAM? IN DARI: "AKRAM KUJA AST?"

?

COLONEL BATTLEFIELD? LET'S GO UPSTAIRS TO THE MEETING ROOM, PLEASE...

AKRAM!

IN DARI: "DAR OTÂG-E MEETING, BÂLA MESHEM."

AKRAM + THE AMERICAN ARMY = ?

YOU WANTED TO SEE US, VAL?

MY CHICKADEES!

WELL DONE, GUYS! B.R.A.V.O.

WE CHECKED OUT YOUR COMIC PAGES. ZIOT MAQBUL AST! SO NOW YOUR WORK IS DONE, I'M GONNA GIVE YOU A PRESENT.

YOU'RE GOING TO BAMIYAN FOR THREE DAYS! A FREE HOLIDAY FROM ZENDAGUI!

IT TAKES ONE DAY TO GET THERE, AND ONE DAY BACK, SO YOU'LL HAVE A FULL DAY.

YOU CAN GO AND TAKE PHOTOS NEXT TO THE GIANT BUDDHAS TO SHOW YOUR FAMILIES.

CHECK YOUR SHOES FOR SCORPIONS EVERY MORNING. IT'S THEIR BREEDING SEASON...

THERE ARE TWO ROADS TO BAMIYAN...

THE SOUTHERN ONE PASSES THROUGH INTER-ETHNIC CONFLICT ZONES...

LANDSLIDES HAVE SHIFTED A MINEFIELD ON THE NORTHERN ONE. SO WATCH OUT.

THE CAR WE'VE HIRED FOR YOU LEAVES YOUR PLACE AT 4 AM TOMORROW. ANY QUESTIONS?

DO WE HAVE TO GO?

EARLY THE NEXT MORNING...

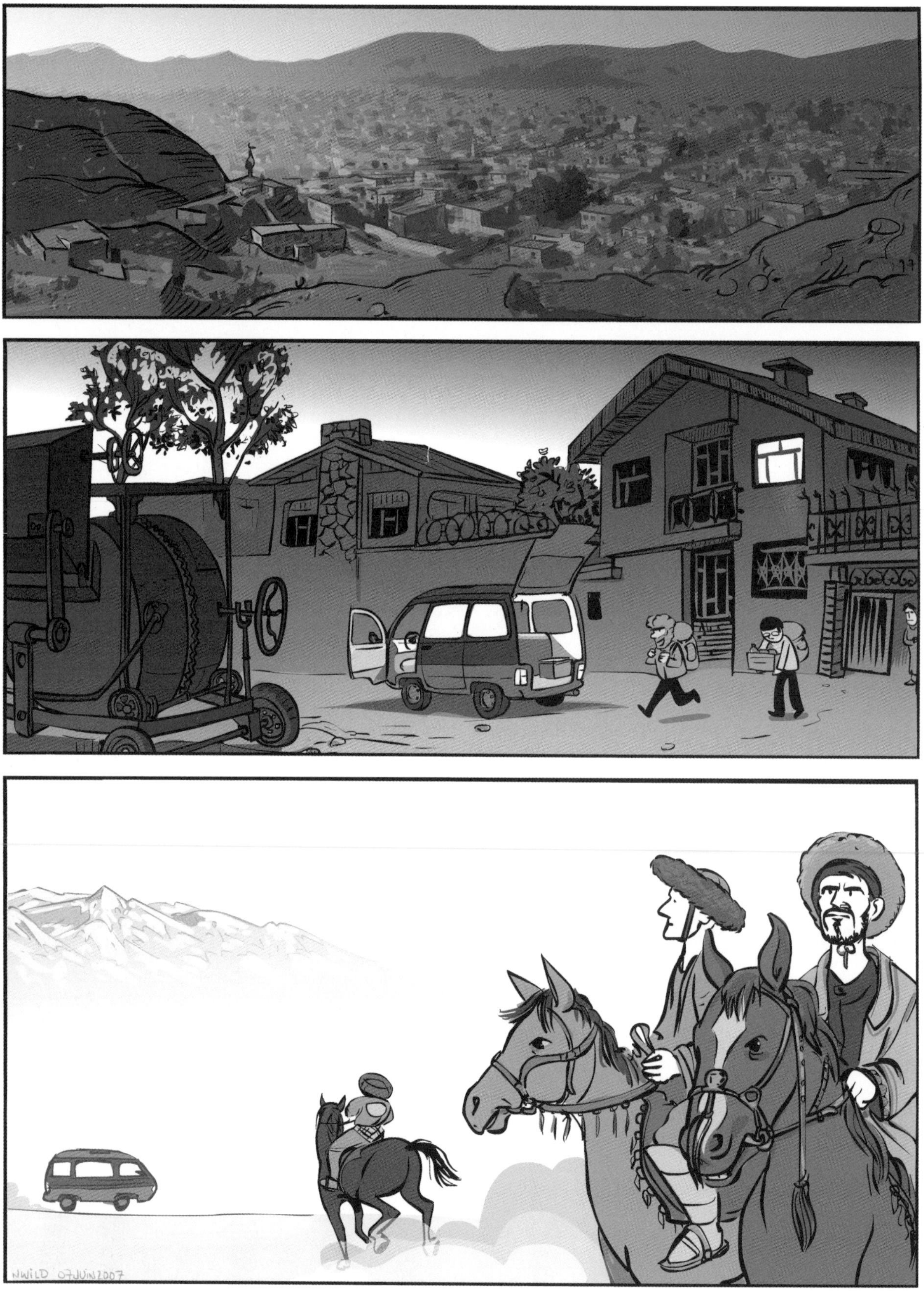
NWILD 07JUIN2007

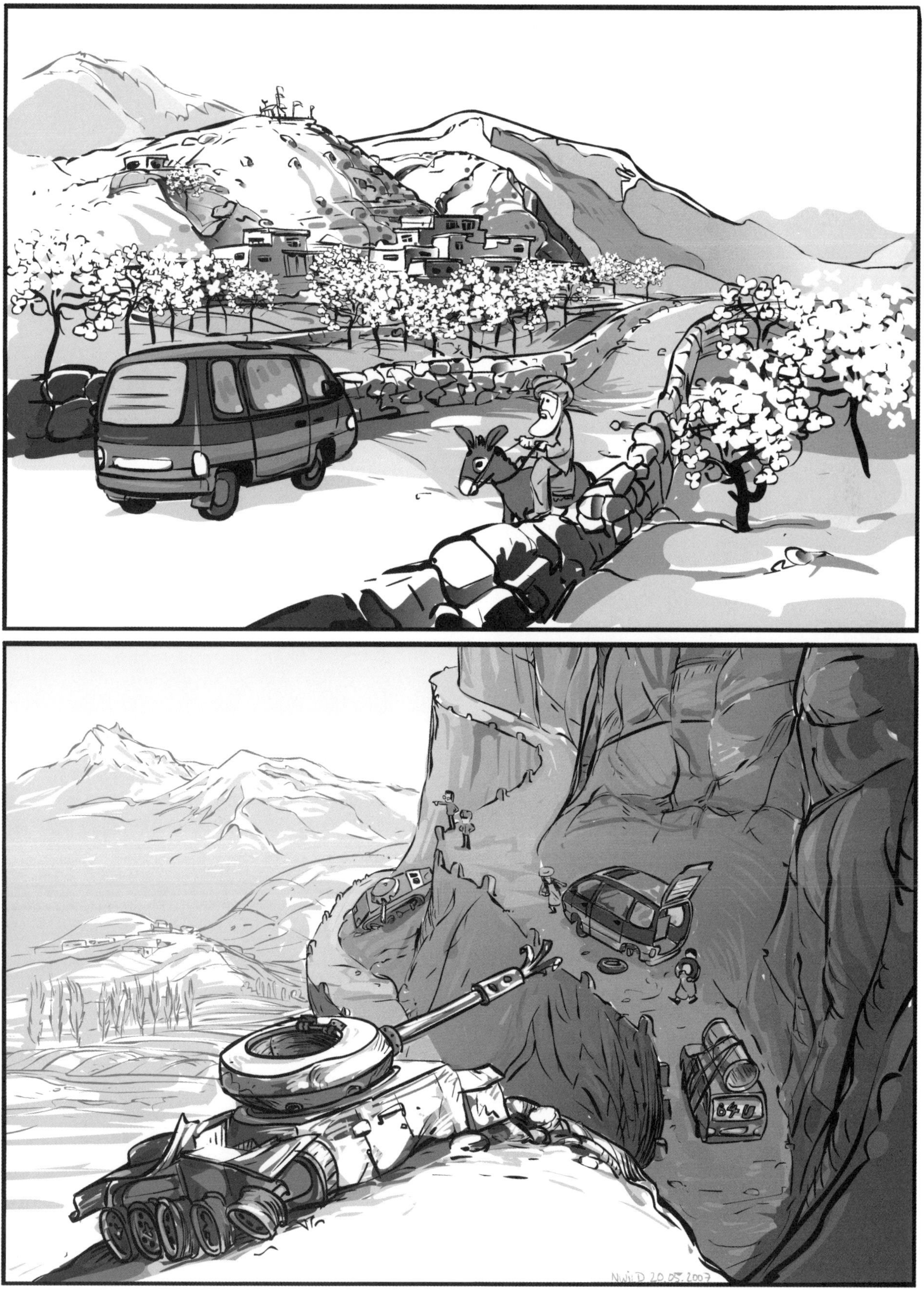
NwiD 20.05.2007

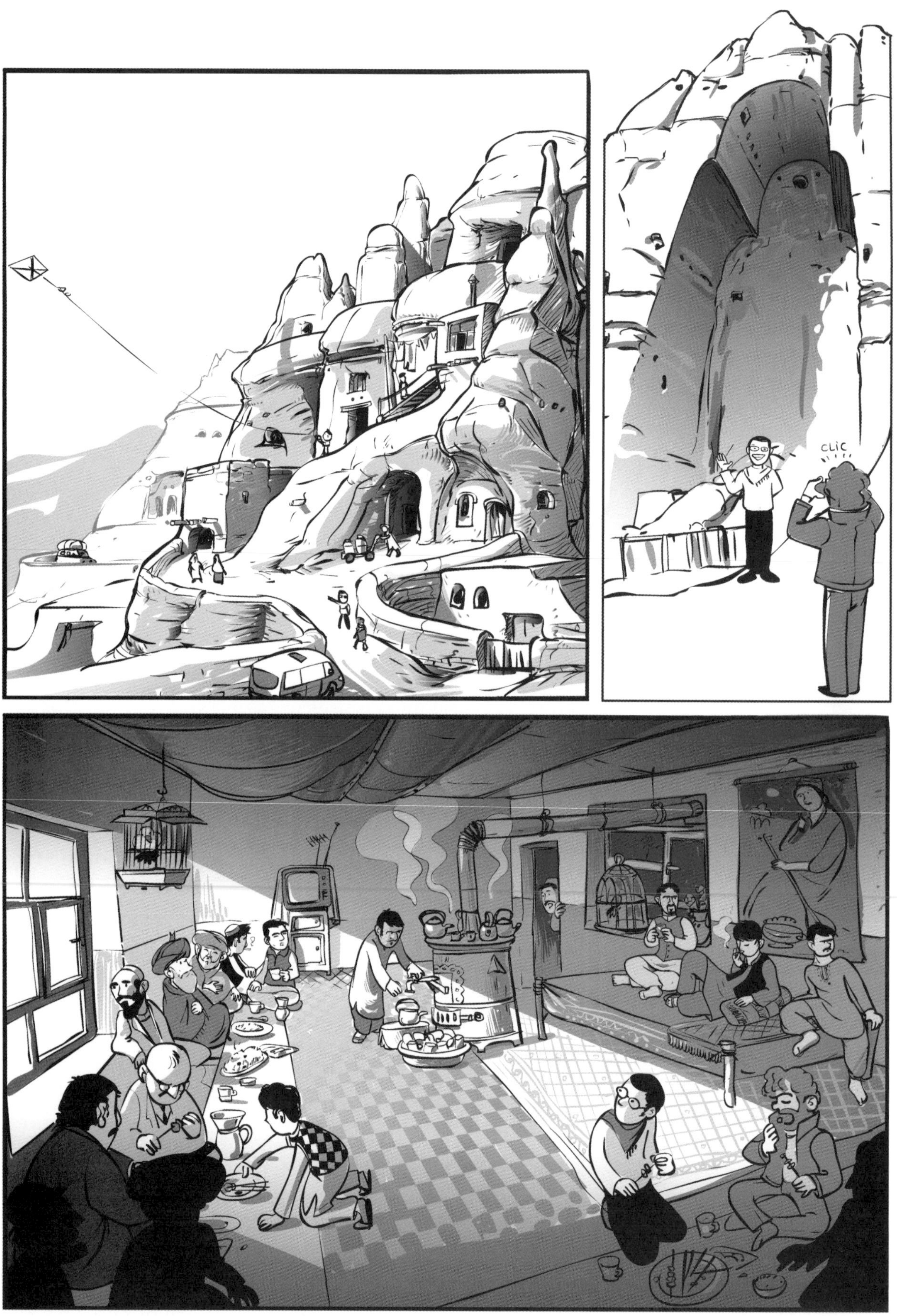
CLIC

THE BAMIYAN VALLEY BOASTS A FASCINATING ARCHAEOLOGICAL HERITAGE. AS WE REACHED THE TOP OF THE ANCIENT "RED CITY" (DESTROYED BY GENGHIS KHAN IN THE 13TH CENTURY*), TRISTAN AND I REALIZED THAT WE'D DONE NO PHYSICAL EXERCISE WHATSOEVER SINCE WE ARRIVED IN AFGHANISTAN.

TOMORROW, I'M QUITTING SMOKING.

TOMORROW, I'M QUITTING WALKING.

*YES, YOU'RE READING AN EDUCATIONAL COMIC!

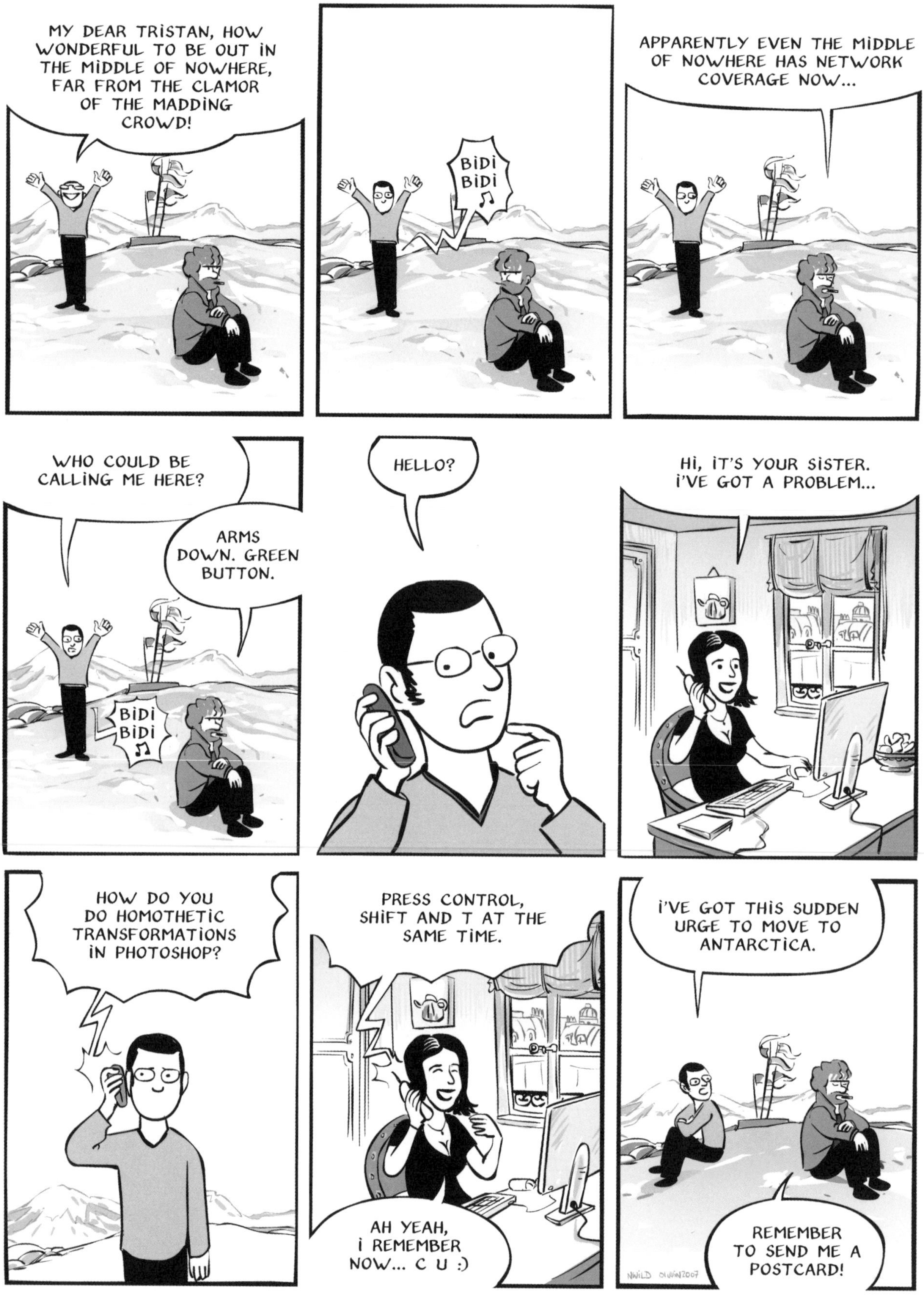
MY DEAR TRISTAN, HOW WONDERFUL TO BE OUT IN THE MIDDLE OF NOWHERE, FAR FROM THE CLAMOR OF THE MADDING CROWD!
BIDI BIDI ♫
APPARENTLY EVEN THE MIDDLE OF NOWHERE HAS NETWORK COVERAGE NOW...
WHO COULD BE CALLING ME HERE?
ARMS DOWN. GREEN BUTTON.
BIDI BIDI ♫
HELLO?
HI, IT'S YOUR SISTER. I'VE GOT A PROBLEM...
HOW DO YOU DO HOMOTHETIC TRANSFORMATIONS IN PHOTOSHOP?
PRESS CONTROL, SHIFT AND T AT THE SAME TIME.
AH YEAH, I REMEMBER NOW... C U :)
I'VE GOT THIS SUDDEN URGE TO MOVE TO ANTARCTICA.
REMEMBER TO SEND ME A POSTCARD!

KNOCK! KNOCK! IT'S ME.

SETTLING DOWN IN YOUR NEW OFFICE?*

YEP!

*ZENDAGUI MOVED INTO NEW BIGGER OFFICES.

BAMIYAN WAS REALLY GORGEOUS! ALMOST MADE ME FEEL LIKE STAYING IN AFGHANISTAN... I'M JUST SAYING... UH...

ANYTHING IN PARTICULAR YOU WANTED TO SAY, NICOLAS?

D'YOU THINK I COULD STAY ON AT ZENDAGUI?

SERIOUSLY?

YEAH, I LIKE WORKING HERE... AT THE START, I THOUGHT YOU WERE ALL KINDA DUMB AND CRAZY...

STILL DO, ACTUALLY...

BUT YOU KNOW...

I DUNNO, NICOLAS. I'LL HAVE TO DISCUSS IT WITH EDOUARD AND DIEGO.

YES, OF COURSE.

OK, BYE!

WHEN A DUCKLING HATCHES FROM AN EGG, IT THINKS THE FIRST LIVING THING IT SEES IS ITS MOTHER...

MOMMY!

VALENTIN SPIDAULT LOVED TO PICK UP EACH NEW ZENDAGUI EMPLOYEE AT THE AIRPORT IN PERSON.

IN LATE MARCH 2005, A BROOD OF THREE NEW EXPATLINGS WAS DUE TO HATCH.

MAUD FESTIVE?

WHO'S THIS HOTTIE?

DUTY FREE

NATHAN BELHOMME?

AS MOLÂQÂT-E BÂ SHOMÂ KHOSH SHODAM, MR. SPIDAULT.*

SHIT! YOU'VE BEEN IN KABUL 5 MINUTES AND SPEAK PERSIAN ALREADY?

I BOUGHT AN ASSIMIL COURSE TWO DAYS AGO.

*PLEASED TO MEET YOU, MR. SPIDAULT.

LÉA BRASILIA?

PLEASE TELL ME YOU'RE MR. SPIDAULT'S SON...

DID DADDY SEND YOU?

MAUD'S A GRAPHIC DESIGNER.

I BROUGHT RED WINE AND A JUNGLE SPEED GAME FROM FRANCE. ANYONE WANT TO PLAY?

NATHAN WILL BE WORKING WITH AZIZ'S TOURING THEATER.

I BROUGHT LE MONDE DIPLOMATIQUE AND COURRIER INTERNATIONAL FROM FRANCE. ANYONE WANT SOME BEDTIME READING?

LÉA WILL BE MONITORING MEDIA COVERAGE.

I BROUGHT A SHITTY CASE OF THE FLU FROM FRANCE. ANYONE GOT ASPIRIN?

APTCHI

BEING SUCH AN OLD HAND, I TOOK IT UPON MYSELF TO SHOW THE NEW KIDS HOW THE HOUSE WORKED.

WHEN THE BULB'S LIT ON THIS THING, IT MEANS WE'VE GOT MAINS ELECTRICITY — THEY CALL IT "CITY POWER" HERE.

WE GET THREE HOURS OF CITY POWER A DAY. USUALLY IN THE EVENING.

WHEN THERE ISN'T ANY, YOU HAVE TO TURN ON THE GENERATOR BY PULLING DOWN THIS LEVER...

GNN

THE GUARD DOES THIS, DON'T WORRY.

THE GROUND-FLOOR TOILET-FLUSHER FLUSHES BADLY...

YOU HAVE TO GIVE IT THREE SHORT PUSHES THEN A LONG ONE...

GORGL-GRL

THEN, TO STOP THE FLOOD, LIFT THE LID AND GRAB THE LITTLE PLASTIC THINGY.

...GORGLOUFLUSH

FINALLY, THE WOOD STOVE. THE BOKHÂRI: BO-KHÂ-RI. DO NOT TRY TO LIGHT IT YOURSELVES WITH NEWSPAPER!!

NO NO NO!

THREE TIMES NO!

THE GUARD WILL LIGHT IT FOR YOU. THE NIGHTS ARE GETTING WARMER ANYWAY...

WHEN I GOT HERE, IT DROPPED TO -20° CELSIUS AT NIGHT!

THAT WAS PRETTY HARSH...

NWLD 12.05.2007

IN THE END, THEY DIDN'T RENEW MY CONTRACT AT ZENDAGUI.

ANYHOW... MY FAMILY IS THROWING ME A HOMECOMING PARTY. THAT SHOULD CHEER ME UP.

HELLO, KITTY-CAT! STILL REMEMBER ME?

WOOF!

COULD'VE SWORN THIS DOOR USED TO OPEN THE OTHER WAY... WEIRD.

YOO-HOO! I'M HOME!

MOM?

NWILD 03.05.2007

62

MY SON! IT'S AWFUL! SINCE YOU LEFT FOR KABUL, THE TALIBAN HAVE SEIZED POWER IN FRANCE...

OH MY GOD! IT'S ALL MY FAULT! WHY DID I EVER LEAVE?

SNIFF

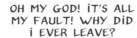

MEOW!

LET ME FINISH STIRRING THE MORTAR. YOUR SISTERS ARE IN THE LIVING ROOM.

BUT HOW WILL I RECOGNIZE THEM IF THEY'RE BOTH WEARING BURQAS?

FRÉDÉRIQUE HAS AN EGG ON HER HEAD.

YOO-HOO! I'M HOME!

THAT'S GOOD NEWS. I NEED YOUR PERMISSION TO GO SWIM IN THE POOL.

63

I THOUGHT I'D START AQUA AEROBICS AGAIN...

BLOOP BLOOP

AAAAAH

WHAT A RIDICULOUS NIGHTMARE! THANK GOD I'M STILL IN KABUL.

PLIC

STILL IN KABUL...

Part Two
NO SPRING IN KABUL

DIEGO, EDOUARD? YOU WANTED TO SEE ME?

TAKE A SEAT!

IT'S STRANGE... EVERY TIME I COME IN, YOUR FURNITURE'S IN DIFFERENT PLACES...

VAL AND I HAVE DIFFERENT FENG SHUI BOOKS...

HERE'S A NEW THREE-MONTH CONTRACT.

REALLY?

WE THINK YOU'VE BEEN WORKING WELL, AND THERE ARE TWO BIG PROJECTS COMING UP. WE'LL BE NEEDING AN EXTRA GRAPHIC DESIGNER.

WHAT PROJECTS ARE THEY?

AS YOU CAN SEE, YOU'LL GET A PAY RISE.

PEN?

YEAH!

ICH BIN EIN KABULER! SO WHAT ARE THESE NEXT PROJECTS?

SIGNING

VALENTIN WILL EXPLAIN. HE'S IN THE MEETING ROOM WITH AKRAM.

BYE!

SNICKER

WE'RE INAUGURATING THE NEW MEETING ROOM TODAY. THESE CHAIRS ARE FROM THE IKEA IN ISLAMABAD.

THE TABLE WAS CUSTOM-MADE FOR US BY AN AFGHAN CARPENTER.

PRETTY HIGH, AS TABLES GO...

WE COULD TURN IT INTO A MEZZANINE!

FINALLY, I'M ALLOWED TO DISCLOSE THE RESULTS OF MY RESEARCH...

DURING THE LAST THREE MONTHS, MY TEAM HAS CRISSCROSSED THE 34 AFGHAN PROVINCES, POLLING OPINIONS ON THE AMERICAN AND AFGHAN ARMIES...

I'M NOT AT LIBERTY TO REVEAL THE RESULTS OF THE POLL ON THE AMERICAN ARMY, BUT THOSE REGARDING THE AFGHAN ARMY WILL BE VITAL TO YOUR NEXT PROJECT.

WHAT NEXT PROJECT?

THE AMERICAN ARMY HAS GIVEN US A CONTRACT TO DEVELOP COMMUNICATIONS FOR THE AFGHAN ARMY'S RECRUITMENT DRIVE.

THIS ARMY WAS CREATED TWO YEARS AGO AND, TO BE EFFICIENT, IT MUST TRIPLE IN SIZE. EVENTUALLY, IT HAS TO ENSURE PUBLIC SECURITY AND MAINTAIN PEACE IN THE COUNTRY.

FOR THE MOMENT, ISAF (INTERNATIONAL SECURITY ASSISTANCE FORCE) SOLDIERS ARE RESPONSIBLE FOR MAINTAINING PEACE IN AFGHANISTAN.

THE ISAF IS MADE UP OF NATO TROOPS FROM NUMEROUS COUNTRIES (THE UK, CANADA, GERMANY, HOLLAND, FRANCE, TURKEY, ITALY, BELGIUM...)

THE AMERICAN ARMY IS HERE TO CONTINUE THE WAR AGAINST THE TALIBAN AND AL-QAEDA.

ENSURING FREEDOM!

THERE ARE STILL A FEW POCKETS OF TALIBAN RESISTANCE IN THE SOUTH.

THE AMERICANS WANT AN EXEMPLARY COMMUNICATIONS CAMPAIGN FOR THE ANA (AFGHAN NATIONAL ARMY). WE'LL BE DOING BRANDING, TO SELL THE AFGHANS A YOUNG, DYNAMIC ARMY THAT PROMISES HOPE FOR A BRIGHT FUTURE.

WE'LL BE PRODUCING 7 POSTERS, 3 STICKERS, 4 TV ADVERTS, 5 RADIO COMMERCIALS, AND INFOMERCIALS FOR THE NEWSPAPERS.

I'M WAITING FOR YOUR IDEAS, MY CHICKADEES!

THE ANA NEEDS YOU!

"DEAR MANAGEMENT, I'M WRITING YOU A LETTER THAT PERHAPS YOU'LL READ, IF YOU HAVE THE TIME.

BELIEVE ME, I HAVE NO WISH TO CREATE MILITARY PROPAGANDA AND PROMOTE WAR.

I DON'T WANT TO DO THIS ANA CAMPAIGN. I WASN'T PUT ON EARTH TO URGE POOR PEOPLE TO ENLIST.

THIS IS NOT INTENDED TO INFURIATE YOU, BUT I'VE DECIDED TO HAND IN MY RESIGNATION."

AFTER THAT SCENE YOU MADE TO GET YOUR CONTRACT RENEWED THE OTHER DAY? HONESTLY...

SKRITCH

GRUMBLE ...

WHAT ARE YOU DOING NOW?

GRUMBLING AND FROWNING!

NAH, I MEANT, D'YOU WANNA HAVE LUNCH WITH ME?

HABIB! DAR RESTAURANT-E FARÂNSAWI MEREM!

SAIST!

IS THE "RESTAURANT-E FARÂNSAWI" CALLED LA JOIE DE VIVRE?

YOU'D RATHER EAT KABULI PILAF?

NAH, I'VE NEVER BEEN THERE, THAT'S ALL...

NO WONDER YOUR SOCIAL LIFE IS NONEXISTENT!

TASHAKOR, HABIB!

La Joie de Vivre
RESTAURANT FRANÇAIS

DON'T BOTHER SEARCHING HIM, HE'S WITH ME.

BIP BIP

SORRY, MR. SPIDAULT, I DIDN'T KNOW.

HELLO, MR. SPIDAULT.

SALÂM!

HELLO, MR. SPIDAULT.

INTER-ETHNIC WARS ARE A SCOURGE IN THIS COUNTRY...

IN THE ANA, ALL THE AFGHAN ETHNICITIES WILL BE MIXED...

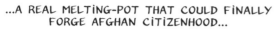

...A REAL MELTING-POT THAT COULD FINALLY FORGE AFGHAN CITIZENHOOD...

FOUR CONSONANTS AND THREE VOWELS MAKE UP THE NAME RAPHAËL ♪♪

WE HAVE TO LET THIS COUNTRY TRY TO GUARANTEE ITS OWN SECURITY...

OK, THE CAMPAIGN'S FUNDED BY THE AMERICAN ARMY...

BUT...

HEY VAL! HOW'S IT GOING?

HEY ENAYAT!

SO ANYWAY, ON ONE SIDE YOU'VE GOT THE ANA, US AND NATO. ON THE OTHER: AL-QAEDA AND THE TALIBAN. WE NEED TO CHOOSE...

I'LL TAKE THE SALAD, PLEASE.

THIS ISN'T THE 70s ANYMORE. IN THIS CONTEXT, BEING A PACIFIST IS JUST POINTLESS...

I DUNNO... IT ALL LOOKS SO COMPLICATED.

HAVE THE CIVET DE BICHE. DELICIOUS! MY TREAT.

AND BRING US A BOTTLE OF POUILLY-FUISSÉ. LOVE THAT STUFF!

CONSIDER IT DONE, HON!

I'M SURE THIS CAMPAIGN WILL BE A GOOD THING FOR THE COUNTRY...

ME TOO...

...I LOVE POUILLY-FUISSÉ...

YOU'VE SEEN THE HUGE PORTRAITS OF MASSOUD IN THE TAJIK NEIGHBORHOODS OF KABUL.

DOESN'T HE LOOK STRONG AND VIRILE, WEARING HIS PAKOL WITH PRIDE?

YES.

ONE DAY, YOU TOO WILL SUBMIT TO THE MASSOUD FASHION.

ONE DAY, YOU'LL TAKE THE PLUNGE...

ONE DAY, YOU'LL BUY A PAKOL.

THEN YOU'LL GO HOME AND HIDE IN THE BATHROOM...

...YOUR NOBLE PURCHASE IN HAND...

...AND NERVOUSLY GET READY TO EXPERIMENT WITH THE BIGGEST FASHION MOMENT OF YOUR LIFE.

AND AS YOU FACE THE MIRROR, YOU'LL SAY...

WHAT A DORK!

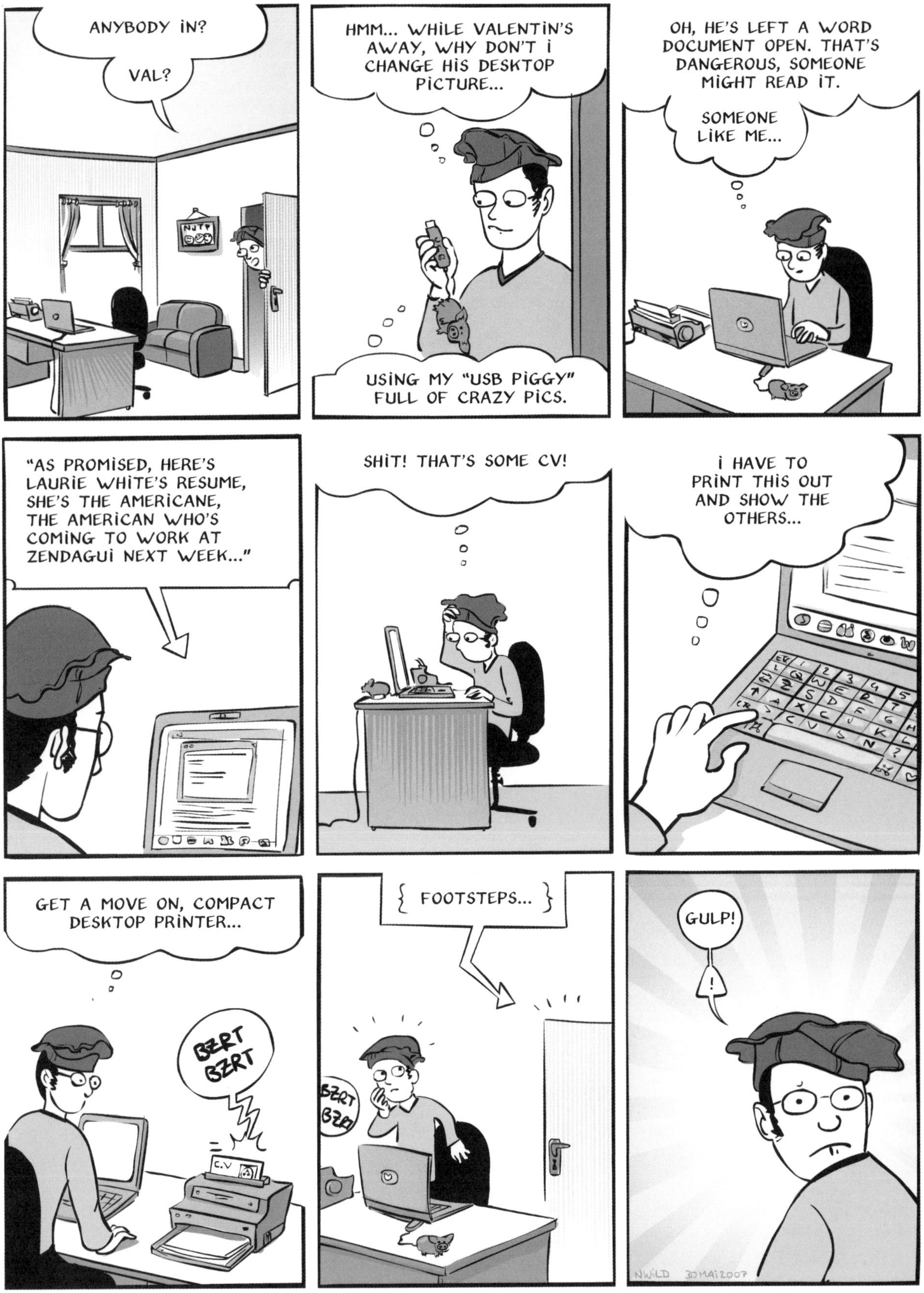
ANYBODY iN?
VAL?
HMM... WHiLE VALENTiN'S AWAY, WHY DON'T i CHANGE HiS DESKTOP PiCTURE...
USiNG MY "USB PiGGY" FULL OF CRAZY PiCS.
OH, HE'S LEFT A WORD DOCUMENT OPEN. THAT'S DANGEROUS, SOMEONE MiGHT READ iT.
SOMEONE LiKE ME...
"AS PROMiSED, HERE'S LAURiE WHiTE'S RESUME, SHE'S THE AMERiCANE, THE AMERiCAN WHO'S COMiNG TO WORK AT ZENDAGUi NEXT WEEK..."
SHiT! THAT'S SOME CV!
i HAVE TO PRiNT THiS OUT AND SHOW THE OTHERS...
GET A MOVE ON, COMPACT DESKTOP PRiNTER...
BZRT BZRT
C.V
{ FOOTSTEPS... }
BZRT BZRT
GULP!
!
NWiLD 30MAi2007

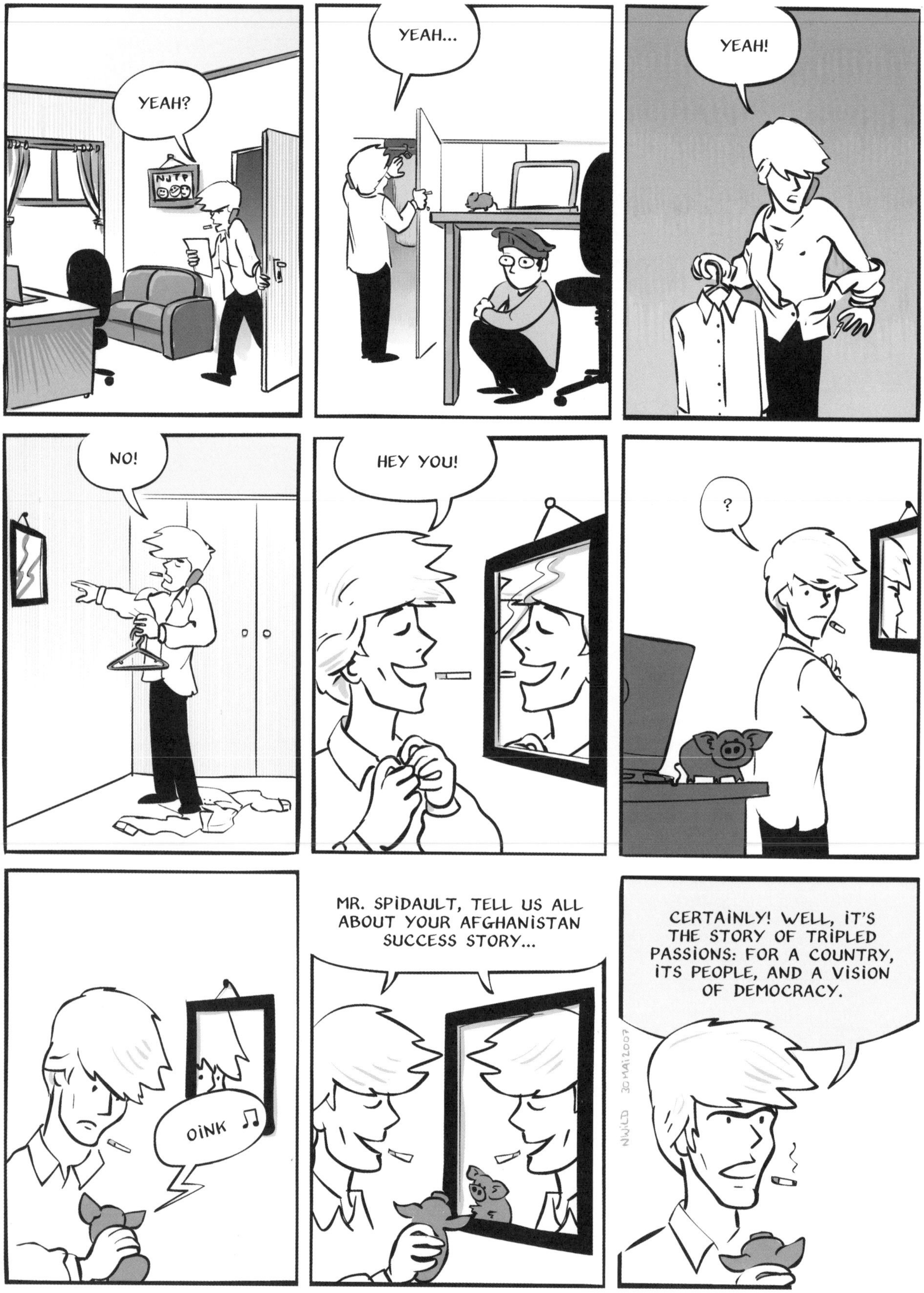

YEAH?
NJTP
YEAH...
YEAH!
NO!
HEY YOU!
?
OINK ♫
MR. SPIDAULT, TELL US ALL ABOUT YOUR AFGHANISTAN SUCCESS STORY...
NWILD 30 MAI 2007
CERTAINLY! WELL, IT'S THE STORY OF TRIPLED PASSIONS: FOR A COUNTRY, ITS PEOPLE, AND A VISION OF DEMOCRACY.

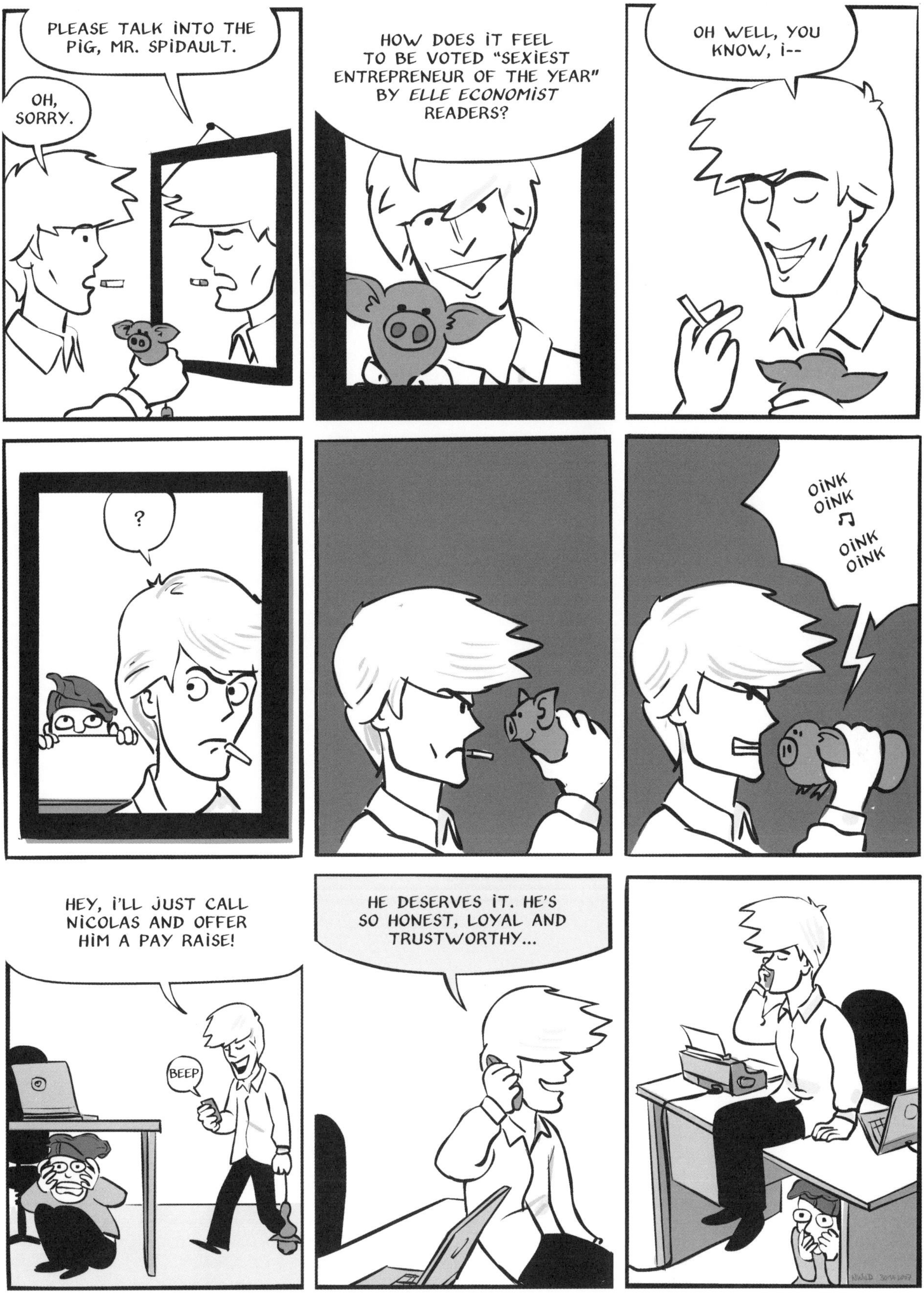
PLEASE TALK INTO THE PIG, MR. SPIDAULT.
OH, SORRY.
HOW DOES IT FEEL TO BE VOTED "SEXIEST ENTREPRENEUR OF THE YEAR" BY *ELLE ECONOMIST* READERS?
OH WELL, YOU KNOW, I--
?
OINK OINK ♫ OINK OINK
HEY, I'LL JUST CALL NICOLAS AND OFFER HIM A PAY RAISE!
BEEP
HE DESERVES IT. HE'S SO HONEST, LOYAL AND TRUSTWORTHY...

BIDI BIDI ♫

BIDI BIDI ♫

ROSHAN ♫ NAZDIK SHODAN...

HELLO, VAL! HAVE YOU GOT MY PIG? I'VE BEEN LOOKING ALL OVER FOR IT...

SORRY, GOTTA GO. THERE'S A *RAT* UNDER MY DESK!

A RAT? MAYBE IT'S HUNGRY? YOU SHOULD TAKE IT TO A RESTAURANT!

TOC TOC

MR. SPIDAULT?

JEAN-FRANÇOIS VOLTAIRE, I'VE COME STRAIGHT FROM THE AIRPORT.

WELCOME ABOARD, MY HEARTY!

FANCY A TOUR O' MY SHIP?

UH, YEAH.

SO, THIS IS MANAGEMENT: EDOUARD, DIEGO AND I WORK IN HERE.

SWEET.

UNDER THE DESK IS NICOLAS, ONE OF MY ILLUSTRATORS...

HELLO ♫

HEY DUDE!

JEAN-FRANÇOIS, RIGHT?

YOU LOOK LIKE AN IDIOT IN THAT PAKOL.

MY FRIENDS CALL ME JEF...

JEF'S A DIRECTOR. HE'S HERE TO FILM TV ADS FOR THE AFGHAN ARMY.

AH.

WHAT'S A PAKOL?

YOU'LL SEE, AFGHANISTAN'S A LAND OF CONTRASTS.

AND, FOR US, A LAND OF CONTRACTS.

HA HA!

WE'RE CHATTERING AWAY, BUT I'VE GOT A COUNTRY TO REBUILD!

DON'T FORGET YOUR PIG!

?

SO, YOU HAVE A GOOD TRIP?

IT WAS KINDA TIRING--

BIDI BIDI ♪♪

YEAH?

...

OINK ♪

APRIL 19TH, 2005

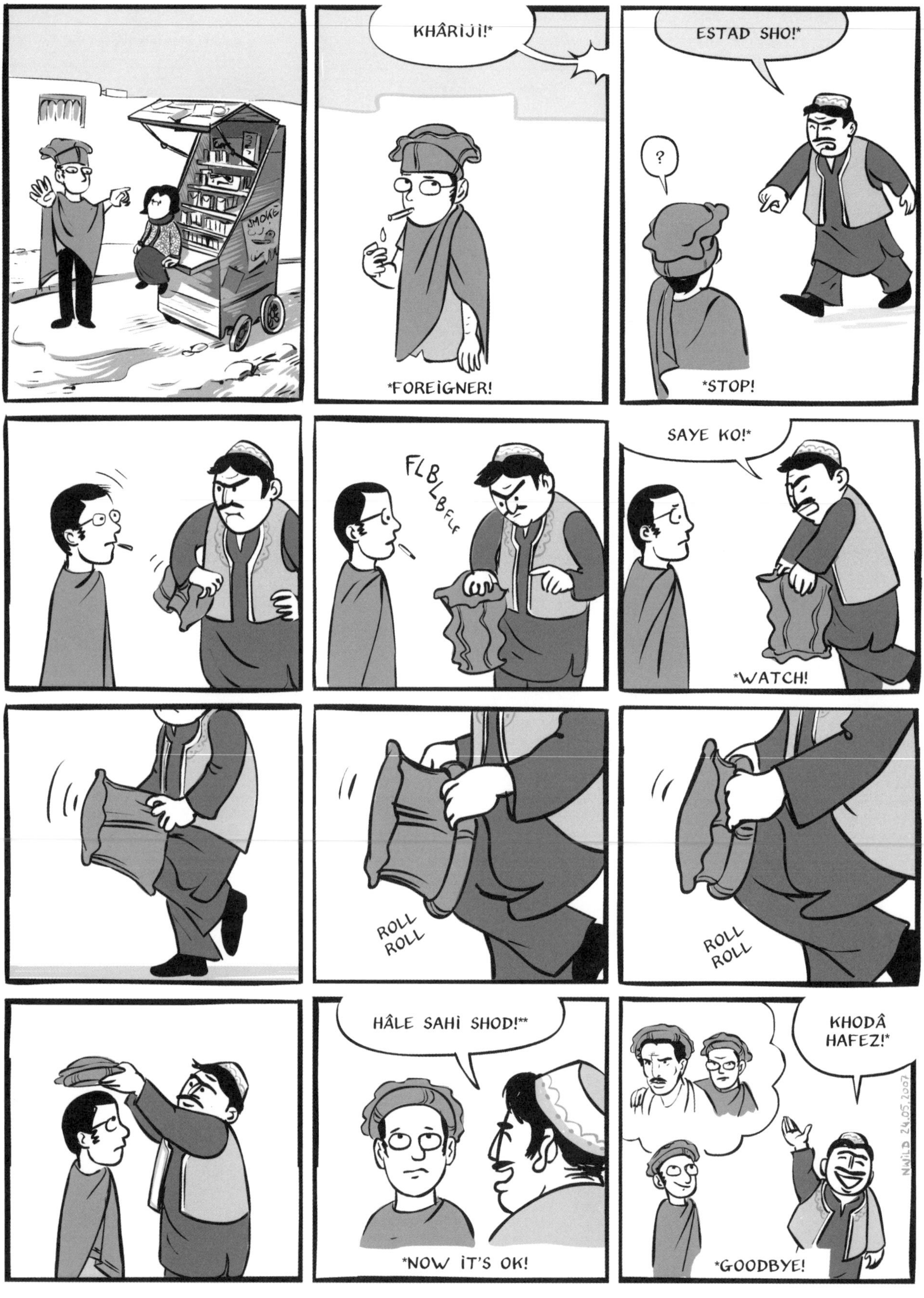
KHÂRIJI!*
*FOREIGNER!
ESTAD SHO!*
?
*STOP!
FLBLBFLF
SAYE KO!*
*WATCH!
ROLL ROLL
ROLL ROLL
HÂLE SAHI SHOD!**
*NOW IT'S OK!
KHODÂ HAFEZ!*
*GOODBYE!

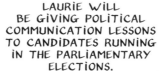

MY CHICKADEES! LET ME INTRODUCE LAURIE WHITE, YOUR NEW COLLEAGUE AND HOUSEMATE.

LAURIE WILL BE GIVING POLITICAL COMMUNICATION LESSONS TO CANDIDATES RUNNING IN THE PARLIAMENTARY ELECTIONS.

HI!

SALÂM!

HELLO!

SO, THIS IS THE GRAPHIC DESIGNERS' OPEN OFFICE...

NICE...

THAT YANK'S A REAL CUTIE-PIE!

READ THIS, IT'LL WIPE THAT SMIRK OFF YOUR FACE.

HER CV? WHERE DID YOU GET IT?

NEVER MIND! HERE...

SHE WORKED ON GEORGE BUSH'S ELECTION CAMPAIGN IN FLORIDA IN NOVEMBER 2000?!

YEP.

HOLY SHIT!

YOU SAID IT!

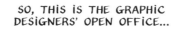

HEY, NEWBIES! THE COOK'S OFF SICK, I'LL TAKE YOU TO A RESTAURANT!

WELCOME TO LA JOIE DE VIVRE! DON'T TELL TRISTAN WE CAME. HE BOYCOTTS THIS PLACE.

TRISTAN'S RIGHT. A LUXURY EXPAT RESTAURANT LIKE THIS IS SCANDALOUS, WHEN YOU THINK HOW MOST AFGHANS DON'T GET ENOUGH TO EAT!

AH...

DO YOU COME HERE OFTEN?

OH NO... HARDLY EVER...

HELLO, MISTER NICOLAS! WILL YOU BE HAVING YOUR USUAL MARTINI APERITIF?

"MISTER" NICOLAS?

SO, TELL ME, MAUD... HOW D'YOU LIKE KABUL?

WILL MISTER NICOLAS TAKE A SLICE OF LEMON IN HIS MARTINI TODAY?

IS ALCOHOL LEGAL HERE?

AND HOW MANY ICE CUBES WOULD YOU LIKE WITH THE SLICE OF LEMON, MISTER NICOLAS?

SO, NATH, HOPE THE JETLAG'S NOT TOO BAD...

WELL NO... I'VE BEEN HERE FOR SIX WEEKS ALREADY...

ANYWAY, WHAT DO YOU RECOMMEND WE EAT HERE?

MISTER NICOLAS ADORES THE VENISON AND CRANBERRY STEW...

HOW EMBARRASSING. THE WAITER MUST THINK I'M SOMEONE ELSE...

HEY! DIEGO!

PHEW!

HAHA! LOOKS LIKE THIS TOWN AIN'T BIG ENOUGH FOR BOTH OF US...

JUST GOT SOME BAD NEWS FROM ANSO.*

WHO'S ANNE-SO?

*ANSO = AFGHAN NGO SAFETY OFFICE.

AN ORGANIZATION THAT SENDS OUT IN-COUNTRY SECURITY INFO. THEY'RE ANTICIPATING TWO SUICIDE ATTACKS ON JALALABAD ROAD BEFORE THE END OF THE MONTH.

WE'LL HAVE TO RESCHEDULE THE ANA* TV AD SHOOT.

HOW COME?

*AFGHAN NATIONAL ARMY (TRY TO REMEMBER IT!)

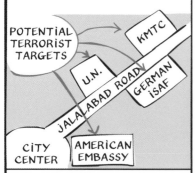

THE SHOOTING LOCATION, KMTC*, IS AT THE FAR END OF JALALABAD ROAD...

POTENTIAL TERRORIST TARGETS

KMTC

U.N.

GERMAN ISAF

JALALABAD ROAD

CITY CENTER

AMERICAN EMBASSY

*KMTC = KABUL MILITARY TRAINING CENTER.

...WHICH MAKES IT A DANGEROUS PLACE TO GET TO. VAL WILL FILL YOU IN THIS AFTERNOON. I'M OFF TO HERAT TOMORROW WITH AZIZ, JORDAN, EDOUARD AND NATHAN. ANY QUESTIONS?

CAN I GO TO HERAT TOO?

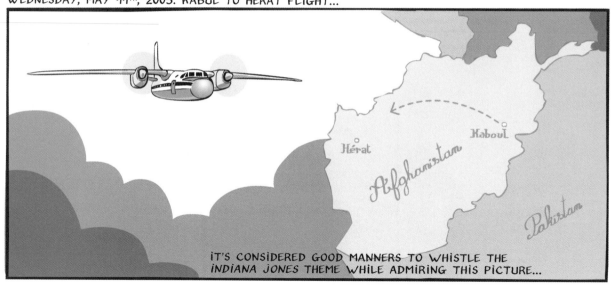

IT'S CONSIDERED GOOD MANNERS TO WHISTLE THE INDIANA JONES THEME WHILE ADMIRING THIS PICTURE...

INITIALLY, IN 2003, ZENDAGUI WAS AN NGO THAT SPECIALIZED IN TRAINING JOURNALISTS (THE NJTP PROGRAM).

BUT WE SOON MOVED INTO CIVIC AND SOCIAL COMMUNICATION PROJECTS: ELECTIONS, LAW, WOMEN'S RIGHTS, HEALTH AND HYGIENE...

SINCE WE WERE GOING BEYOND OUR ORIGINAL REMIT, WE DECIDED TO SET UP A PRIVATE COMPANY. ZENDAGUI MEDIA AND COMMUNICATION WAS BORN ON 6 DECEMBER, 2004.

WHY ARE YOU TAKING NOTES? YOU WRITING A NOVEL ABOUT ZENDAGUI?

ME? NO, NO.

MOST OF THE FOREIGNERS HERE WRITE ABOUT THEIR LIVES.

AS IF THE KABUL AIR GIVES THEM WRITING SKILLS...

JUST IMAGINE NICOLAS' NOVEL! CHAPTER ONE: "HOW I GOT STUCK IN AZERBAIJAN..."

HA HA HA!

HAHA...

ZENDAGUI IS CELEBRATING TWO EVENTS IN HERAT TODAY. FOR STARTERS, THE NJTP'S FIRST ANNIVERSARY. DIEGO AND PROFESSOR NASRULLAH (WHO RUNS THE NJTP IN HERAT) ARE DELIVERING SPEECHES TO THE JOURNALISM ALUMNAE.

AND THEN THE PREVIEW OF AZIZ'S PLAY ABOUT PARLIAMENTARY ELECTIONS. THE AUDIENCE IS GIVEN COMPLIMENTARY ICE CREAM.

ER, AZIZ? WHAT ARE THEY SAYING?

THE GUY IN THE HAT HAS COME TO THE VILLAGE TO ANNOUNCE THE ELECTIONS. THE PERSIAN WORD FOR "PARLIAMENT" CAN ALSO MEAN "WRESTLING"...

THIS CONFUSES THE TOWN CRIER, WHO ANNOUNCES A NATIONAL WRESTLING CONTEST! THE VILLAGE MECHANIC VOLUNTEERS...

EVERYTHING GETS BACK TO NORMAL WHEN THE VILLAGE ELDER'S WIFE EXPLAINS THE REAL POINT...

WE DO SOME SIGHTSEEING IN THE AFTERNOON...

VISITING THE CITADEL...

THE GREAT MOSQUE...

SUNSET OVER PUL-E MALAN BRIDGE...

MY COLLEAGUES LEAVE THE NEXT DAY. I STAY ON FOR TWO MORE DAYS TO DO SOME SKETCHING IN TOWN.

TODAY IS MY BIRTHDAY. IT'S ALSO THE FIRST DAY I'VE SPENT ON MY OWN SINCE ARRIVING IN AFGHANISTAN, GIVING ME AN UNPRECEDENTED SENSE OF FREEDOM...

SALÂM ALEIKUM! CHAI BOKHO?*

*HELLO! WANT SOME TEA?

IN AFGHANISTAN, OFFERING SOMEONE A CUP OF TEA IS JUST GOOD MANNERS, AND ONE SHOULD REPLY: "NO THANK YOU, I'VE JUST HAD ONE. STAY ALIVE!"

TEA? OH YES!

IF AN AFGHAN REALLY DOES WANT TO GIVE YOU TEA, HE'LL OFFER IT FOUR MORE TIMES. ONLY THEN MAY YOU SAY: "OH, YES PLEASE. I AM KINDA THIRSTY..."

I KNEW NOTHING OF ALL THIS, SO HOW MANY GALLONS OF TEA HAD I IMPOLITELY IMBIBED DUE TO MY IGNORANCE OF AFGHAN CUSTOMS?

OH, BESYÂR KHUB AST!* HA HA HA!

PFFT.

*OH, IT'S VERY GOOD!

DOKHTAR-E MA RASEM MIKONI?*

ALRIGHT THEN.

*CAN YOU DRAW MY DAUGHTER?

ONE HOUR LATER...

BIDI BIDI

HAPPY BIRTHDAY!

WHO IS IT?

FRIENDS CALLING FROM FRANCE (ERWANN AND ESTELLE*) TO WISH ME A HAPPY BIRTHDAY. HOW KIND OF THEM.

*I'VE PUT YOU IN MY COMIC, SO YOU OWE ME A BEER NOW!

AGAIN?

BIDI BIDI

NICOLAS, DID YOU HEAR ABOUT GUANTÁNAMO?

ER...

LAST WEEK, NEWSWEEK REVEALED THAT AMERICAN SOLDIERS HAD ALLEGEDLY DESECRATED THE QUR'ĀN IN FRONT OF PRISONERS.

OH, I THOUGHT YOU WERE CALLING FOR MY BIRTHDAY...

THAT DESECRATION HAS SPARKED DEMONSTRATIONS IN SEVERAL MUSLIM COUNTRIES, ESPECIALLY AFGHANISTAN.

YESTERDAY IN JALALABAD, A STUDENT PROTEST TURNED INTO A RIOT. POLICE FIRED INTO THE CROWD, KILLING THREE AND INJURING OTHERS...

BLOUP

BLOUP

OH WOW! ARE THERE PROTESTS IN KABUL?

NOT YET, BUT SIMILAR DEMONSTRATIONS ARE PLANNED IN HERAT TODAY.

WHAT?

GET TO THE HIF* GUESTHOUSE. YOU'LL BE SAFE THERE.

BUT...I DON'T KNOW WHERE IT IS!

*HANDICAP INTERNATIONAL FRANCE.

JUMP IN A CAB AND CALL ME. I'LL TELL THE DRIVER WHERE TO GO.

OK.

DON'T PANIC.

KHODÂ HAFEZ! THANKS FOR THE TEA!

JUST MY LUCK.

WAIT...

I...I'M LOST!

AND THEN?

AFTER MANY ADVENTURES, I MADE IT TO HiF...

HELLO! ♫

DO I KNOW YOU?

I'M A FRIEND OF DIEGO'S.

OH.

RUMBLINGS OF DEMONSTRATIONS THAT AFTERNOON THREW THEIR NEW HEAD OF SECURITY INTO MAJOR PANIC.

TO LIGHTEN THINGS UP, I SAID:

IT'S MY BIRTHDAY!

THAT EVENING, THE STAFF AT HiF BOUGHT ME A CAKE.

OH!

AFTER SPENDING THE WHOLE DAY WITH THEM, IT FELT LIKE I'D KNOWN THEM FOREVER...

I WAS TOUCHED, AND SANG THEM A SONG TO THANK THEM FOR THEIR HOSPITALITY.

OK, BUT WHAT ABOUT THE PROTESTS?

WHAT?

THERE WEREN'T ANY IN THE END...

GUYS! THERE'S A COOL CONCERT ON AT THE AFC* TONIGHT!

*AFGHAN FOUNDATION FOR CULTURE.

YOU'RE GONNA LOVE IT!

F.C.A

FRIENDS OF AFGHAN CULTURE, LET'S HEAR A HUGE ROUND OF APPLAUSE FOR THE GREAT POET AND SETAR PLAYER, MANDA BUSHI!

CLAP. CLAP. CLAP. CLAP.

THANK YOU. TASHAKOR. MAY I POINT OUT THAT I STUDIED MUSIC THEORY IN STUTTGART.

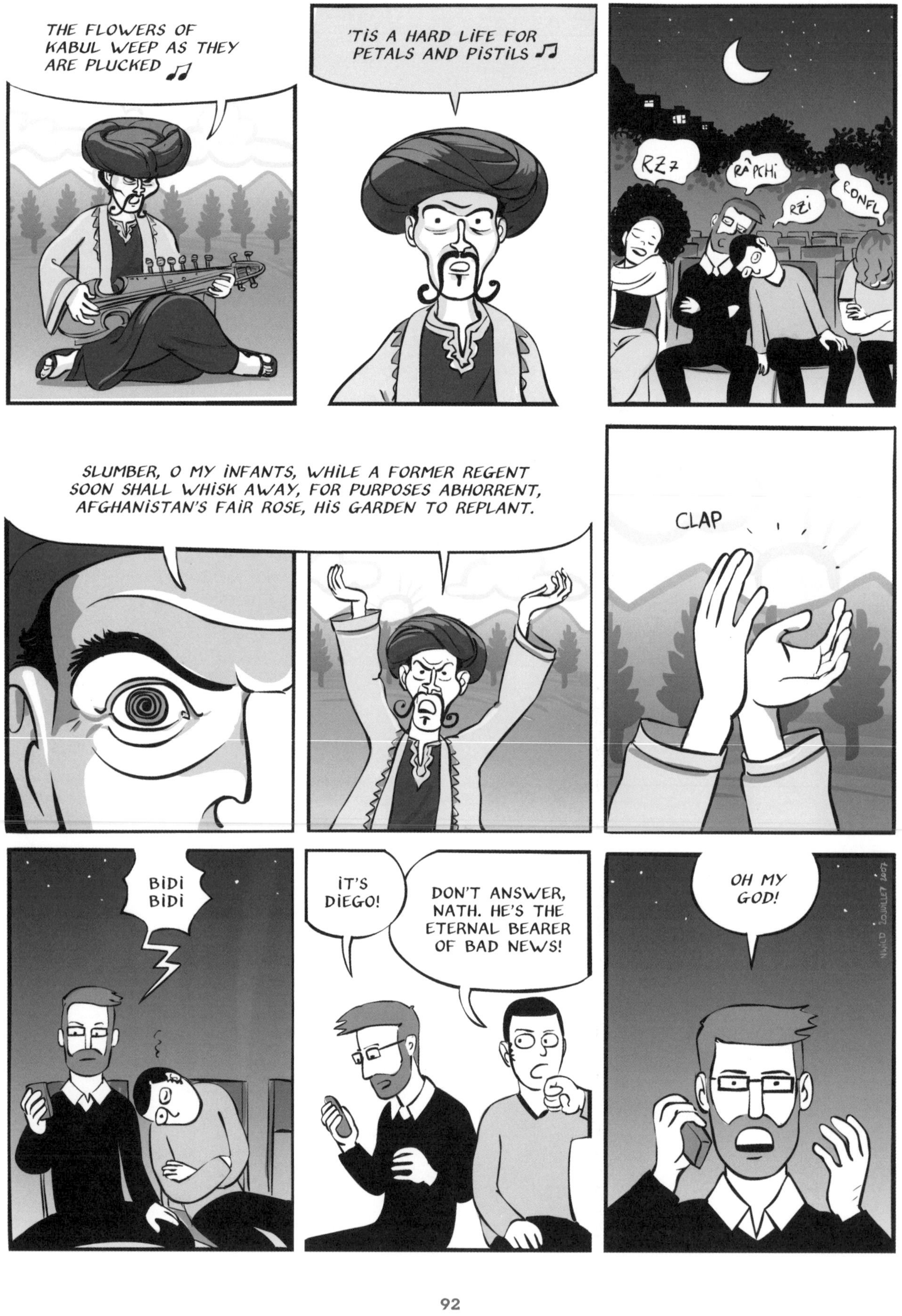
THE FLOWERS OF KABUL WEEP AS THEY ARE PLUCKED
'TIS A HARD LIFE FOR PETALS AND PISTILS
SLUMBER, O MY INFANTS, WHILE A FORMER REGENT SOON SHALL WHISK AWAY, FOR PURPOSES ABHORRENT, AFGHANISTAN'S FAIR ROSE, HIS GARDEN TO REPLANT.
CLAP
BIDI BIDI
IT'S DIEGO!
DON'T ANSWER, NATH. HE'S THE ETERNAL BEARER OF BAD NEWS!
OH MY GOD!

THERE'S BEEN A KIDNAPPING IN OUR DISTRICT!

A KIDNAPPING?!

YES! A KIDNAPPING!

WHERE ARE YOU? I'M COMING TO GET YOU.

FIVE MINUTES LATER...

...DIEGO DRIVES US BACK TO THE GUESTHOUSE.

STAY TOGETHER IN THE LOUNGE. DON'T TURN ON THE GENERATOR.

I'LL GIVE THE GUARDS THEIR INSTRUCTIONS. BACK SOON.

DON'T WORRY, DIEGO KNOWS WHAT HE'S DOING...

NWILD 26.JUILLET 2007

93

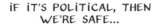

WE NEED TO FIND OUT FAST WHETHER THIS KIDNAPPING'S THE FIRST IN A SERIES ORGANIZED BY A CRIMINAL GANG...

...OR WHETHER IT'S A POLITICAL ABDUCTION.

IF IT'S POLITICAL, THEN WE'RE SAFE...

OH? HOW COME?

REMEMBER THAT ENGLISH GUY WHO GOT ASSASSINATED LAST MARCH?

APPARENTLY HE TRIED TO CONDEMN SEVERAL POLITICAL FIGURES IMPLICATED IN OPIUM TRAFFICKING.

BLAM

HE WAS A *POLITICAL* TARGET...

BUT NONE OF ZENDAGUI'S EMPLOYEES CAN BE CONSIDERED POLITICAL TARGETS BECAUSE OF THEIR WORK IN THIS COUNTRY...

NONE EXCEPT FOR--

HI GUYS!

LAURIE WHITE!!!

FINALLY, SOMEONE'S BEEN KIDNAPPED! PHEW! I ALMOST FEEL RELIEVED!

I BROUGHT SOME BEERS FROM THE LEBANESE RESTAURANT. HELP YOURSELVES.

GLUG

WHAT? NEVER SEEN ME DRINKING BEER BEFORE?

GLUG

LAURIE... THERE'S SOMETHING WE'VE ALL BEEN WONDERING ABOUT...

?

WHAT WAS YOUR ROLE IN THE 2000 U.S. PRESIDENTIAL ELECTIONS?

HA HA HA!!!

I KNEW YOU WERE GONNA ASK ME THAT...

I'LL TELL YOU ABOUT IT...

BACK THEN, I WAS WORKING FOR THE REPUBLICAN PARTY. I WAS RESPONSIBLE FOR VOTE-COUNTING IN ONE OF FLORIDA'S THREE PROVINCES...

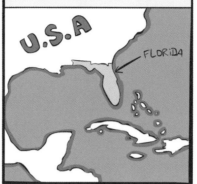

U.S.A

FLORIDA

WE DIDN'T HAVE THE FINAL RESULTS YET BECAUSE, DUE TO THE TIME ZONE, THE POLLS IN THE WEST OF THE PROVINCE CLOSED AN HOUR LATER...

BUSH PRESIDE

BUT MEANWHILE, ON TV...

THE RESULTS FOR FLORIDA ARE JUST IN...

IT'S OFFICIAL, THE STATE HAS SWUNG TO THE LEFT...

TOX NEWS channel

AL GORE HAS WON THE ELECTION...

THE DEMOCRATS ARE JUBILANT...

FUCK!

MISS WHITE! THEY'VE GOT TO BE WRONG! THOSE RESULTS AREN'T FINAL!

WHAT DO WE DO?

I CALLED MY BOSS IMMEDIATELY...

HE WAS LIVE IN THE STUDIO...

NT CLINTON/
CONGRATULATED
FOR THE FUTURE
HIS WIFE...

BIDI BIDI

TOX NEWS channel

HELLO? LAURIE? ARE YOU SURE? ALL OUR JOBS ARE ON THE LINE IF THIS REPORT'S WRONG...

i...

i WAS IN A DAZE... THE WHOLE THING COULD'VE COLLAPSED RIGHT THERE...

MR. FISHER, WHAT'S YOUR ANALYSIS OF FLORIDA'S DEMOCRATIC SWING?

THE DEMOCRATS TOOK FLORIDA? ARE YOU *SURE*?

TOX NEWS channel

HOW CAN YOU SAY THAT WHILE SOME POLLING STATIONS ARE STILL OPEN?

DON'T COUNT YOUR ELEPHANTS...*

*NOTE: THE ELEPHANT IS THE REPUBLICAN PARTY'S MASCOT.

i'M GONNA KEEP THIS PHONE ALL MY LIFE TO REMIND ME OF THIS MOMENT...

WHEN THEY HEARD THE NEWS, VOTERS WHO HADN'T YET VOTED RUSHED TO POLLING STATIONS THAT WERE STILL OPEN...

THE RESULTS WERE SO CLOSE THAT A STATEWIDE VOTE RECOUNT WOULD HAVE BEEN REQUIRED.

14,983... 14,984... 14,985... 14,986...

BUT THE (MOSTLY REPUBLICAN) SUPREME COURT DECIDED TO SUSPEND THE TEDIOUS RECOUNT...

AND IN THE END, FLORIDA STAYED REPUBLICAN.

U.S.A

IF I HADN'T CALLED, GEORGE W. BUSH WOULD NEVER HAVE GOT IN...

WHEN YOU POUR ALL YOUR ENERGY INTO A POLITICAL PARTY 24/7 FOR SEVERAL MONTHS...

...BEING DECLARED THE WINNER IS LIKE AN ORGASM! I CAN'T DESCRIBE HOW IT FEELS...

...IT'S BETTER THAN SEX!!!

NO DOUBT ABOUT IT!

THERE YOU GO... BUT DO WE HAVE ANY IDEA WHO'S BEEN KIDNAPPED YET?

YES.

DIEGO!!!

HER NAME IS CLEMENTINA CANTONI.

CLEMENTINA WHAT?

WHO'S SHE?

DO YOU KNOW HER?

IT HAPPENED ABOUT THREE HOURS AGO, ON 2ND STREET, TAIMANI...

...AS SHE WAS ON HER WAY HOME.

ARMED MEN RAN OUT OF THE SHADOWS...

...AND FORCED HER TO GET INTO THEIR CAR.

CLEMENTINA'S COLLEAGUES AND DRIVER WERE POWERLESS TO STOP THEM...

WHO WAS CLEMENTINA WORKING FOR?

FOR THE CARE INTERNATIONAL NGO, HELPING AFGHAN WIDOWS REINTEGRATE INTO SOCIETY.

AFGHAN WIDOWS? SO THIS IS DEFINITELY A POLITICAL ABDUCTION!

HA HA!

SHUT UP!!!

GO TO BED! ALL OF YOU! I'M DOUBLING THE NUMBER OF GUARDS OUTSIDE YOUR GUESTHOUSE TONIGHT.

SECURITY BRIEFING AT THE OFFICE FIRST THING IN THE MORNING.

DIEGO? DID YOU KNOW THIS CLEMENTINA?

YES... SHE'S A FRIEND...

IS EVERYONE HERE?

EVERY FOREIGN ORGANIZATION IN KABUL SETS OUT ITS OWN SECURITY RULES.

HERE AT ZENDAGUI, I'M HEAD OF SECURITY.

FIRST, I'M GOING TO CHECK IF YOU'VE ALL READ THE BASIC SECURITY RULES YOU WERE GIVEN ON ARRIVAL IN AFGHANISTAN.

MAUD, WHAT DO YOU DO BEFORE PUTTING ON YOUR SHOES IN THE MORNING?

UM...

PUT MY SOCKS ON?

NO!

YOU SHOULD CHECK THERE ARE NO SCORPIONS IN THERE FIRST!

DID YOU KNOW, JEF?

HUH, I DON'T CARE... I SLEEP WITH MY SHOES ON...

LET'S PRACTICE A FEW DARI PHRASES THAT'LL BE HANDY FOR GETTING OUT OF A TIGHT SPOT.

HOW DO YOU SAY "I'M HUNGRY"?

GOSHNA HASTAM!

GOOD, NICOLAS. HOW DO YOU SAY "I'M THIRSTY"?

TOSHNA HASTAM!

HOW DO YOU SAY "PLEASE, CAN YOU TELL ME WHERE THE FRENCH EMBASSY IS?"

LUTFAN, SHOMÂ MEFÂMED SIFÂRAT-E FARÂNSA-YE DAR KUJÂ AST?

BROWN-NOSER...

GREAT, NATHAN. THERE ARE MORE PHRASES ON THESE CARDS... PASS THEM ROUND.

NWILD 23 JUIN 2007

102

AS OF LAST NIGHT, WE'VE GONE UP TO SECURITY LEVEL 2!

SECURITY LEVEL 2?

YES! SECURITY LEVEL 2!

SECURITY LEVEL 1
AFGHANISTAN'S A COOL PLACE. YOU CAN EVEN GO OUT IN THE STREETS TO BUY CIGARETTES.

SECURITY LEVEL 2
YIKES, THE SITUATION IN THE COUNTRY'S KINDA ROUGH. I'D BE BETTER OFF STAYING AT HOME AND SENDING THE GUARD OUT FOR CIGARETTES.

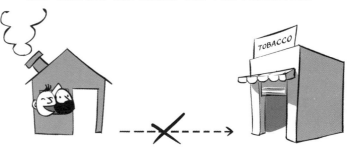

SECURITY LEVEL 3
WE ALL STAY AT HOME AND PRAY TO GOD THAT NOBODY'S TOUCHED THE LEVEL 3 CIGARETTE SUPPLY. THE WORSE THING ABOUT ALL THIS IS THAT, THE HIGHER THE SECURITY LEVEL, THE LESS YOU WANT TO QUIT SMOKING.

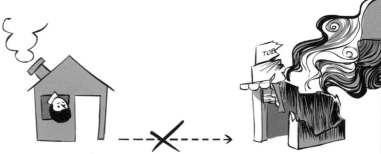

SECURITY LEVEL 4
IN THEORY, YOU SHOULD ALREADY HAVE BEEN REPATRIATED TO FRANCE. THE TOBACCO SHOP WAS BOMBED ANYWAY, AND THE GUARD'S BEEN TEMPORARILY LAID OFF.

NWILD 23 JUIN 2007

FROM NOW ON, NO ONE'S ALLOWED OUT OF THE GUESTHOUSE, EXCEPT TO GO TO THE OFFICE...

EVERY DAY, A TWO-VEHICLE CONVOY WITH GUARDS WILL LEAVE AT 8 AM SHARP TO DRIVE YOU TO THE OFFICE.

NO MORE GOING HOME AT LUNCH TIME. WE'LL EAT AT THE OFFICE WITH OUR AFGHAN COLLEAGUES.

CAN I FINISH THE KABULI?

AT 5:30 PM, THE CONVOY WILL TAKE YOU BACK HOME.

AT 6 PM, TWILIGHT BEGINS AND THE CURFEW STARTS.

ALLAHU AKBAR ♪

NO ONE IS TO LEAVE THE GUESTHOUSE UNTIL MORNING.

I'M BORED!

WE'LL BUY YOU SOME DVDS AND BOARD GAMES.

MY PROPERTY! YOU OWE ME 5,000 AFGHANIS.

SHIT! LET'S WATCH A DVD INSTEAD!

A SURVIVAL CHEST FULL OF FOOD AND SMOKES WILL BE STORED IN THE KITCHEN. IT IS NOT TO BE OPENED UNTIL SECURITY LEVEL 3.

WE'LL ALSO GIVE YOU A SATELLITE PHONE TO BE USED ONLY IN EXTREME EMERGENCIES...

DEAR BLOG, SINCE ARRIVING IN KABUL, THE ATMOSPHERE IN THE COUNTRY HAS REALLY GONE DOWNHILL!

THE TALIBAN RESISTANCE HAS BEEN FIERCER THAN EXPECTED...

THERE HAVE BEEN OTHER ATTEMPTED ABDUCTIONS IN OUR DISTRICT, ONE OF THEM OUTSIDE *LA JOIE DE VIVRE*.

IT'S NOW OFF-LIMITS TO MOST FOREIGNERS (US INCLUDED).

WHY DOES HE PUT SO MUCH OIL IN THE FOOD?

AFGHAN CUISINE MEANS GREASE GALORE...

CLAUSTROPHOBIA AND PARANOIA HAVE BECOME OUR STANDARD OPERATING PROCEDURE.

LÉA SLEEPS WITH A KNIFE UNDER HER PILLOW.

SNORE

IT'S LIKE WE'RE LIVING IN A REALITY TV SHOW.

WELCOME TO *BIG BROTHER KABUL!*

WE'VE LOCKED SIX ANTI-BUSH FRENCH AND ONE PRO-BUSH AMERICAN IN A HOUSE.

YOU CAN PHONE IN TO CHOOSE WHICH CONTESTANT GETS KIDNAPPED FIRST.

TO HAVE LAURIE WHITE ABDUCTED, DIAL 911 ON YOUR CELL PHONE...

DIAL 911

AFTER TEN DAYS OF LIVING THIS WAY, WE STARTED MISSING SIMPLE THINGS LIKE GOING FOR A WALK.

IN THE EVENING, WHEN HE GOT BACK FROM THE OFFICE, AKRAM WOULD WALK AROUND THE GARDEN A FEW TIMES...

MEANWHILE, CLEMENTINA WAS ALWAYS IN THE NEWS. THE ANTI-TALIBAN HEAD OF THE ISLAMIC COUNCIL IN KANDAHAR PROVINCE, MULLAH FAYAZ, CONDEMNED HER KIDNAPPING...

THIS DESPICABLE ACT INSULTS OUR RELIGIOUS VALUES.

CAN I WALK WITH YOU?

YES, BUT IN SILENCE.

THE TALIBAN WEREN'T KEEN ON THE MULLAH'S SPEECH.

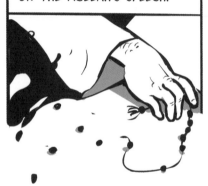

FAYAZ WAS KILLED IN AN ATTACK THE NEXT DAY...

ON THE MORNING OF JUNE 1ST, A PRAYER CEREMONY FOR THE MULLAH'S DEATH WAS HELD IN A KANDAHAR MOSQUE...

SEVERAL HUNDRED AFGHANS FLOCKED TO PAY THEIR LAST RESPECTS TO THE RELIGIOUS LEADER.

AMONG THEM WAS A TALIBAN SUICIDE BOMBER.

THIS SECOND ATTACK KILLED TWENTY AND INJURED ANOTHER FIFTY.

ON JUNE 3RD, WE STARTED GARDENING...

GREAT NEWS! THE ANA ADVERTISING SHOOT IS FINALLY HAPPENING. WHICH ONE OF YOU FOUR'S GOING WITH JEF TO TAKE PHOTOS FOR THE POSTERS?

I NEED TO FINISH THE PROGRAM FOR THE NJTP PHOTO EXHIBITION.

I NEED TO FINISH THE ILLUSTRATIONS FOR THE BOOKLET ON PARLIAMENTARY ELECTIONS.

I'M WORKING ON THE MINISTRY OF EDUCATION'S LOGO.

UH...

CATCH!

SHOULD HAVE SPOKEN UP SOONER...

BUT... UH... IS THERE STILL A RISK OF SUICIDE ATTACKS ON JALALABAD ROAD?

IF YOU'RE NOT INTO DANGER, GO BACK TO FRANCE.

WELCOME ON BOARD, DUDE!

SALÂM!

THE FILMING LOCATION...

KMTC, AT THE END OF JALALABAD ROAD...

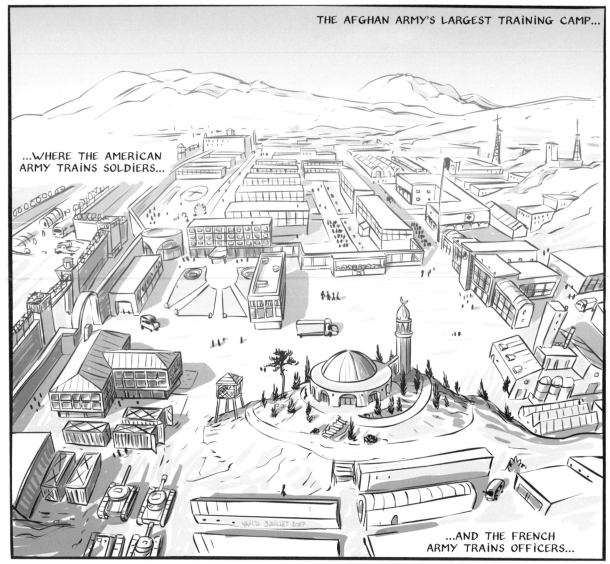

THE AFGHAN ARMY'S LARGEST TRAINING CAMP...

...WHERE THE AMERICAN
ARMY TRAINS SOLDIERS...

...AND THE FRENCH
ARMY TRAINS OFFICERS...

COLONEL SHAPUR'S IN CHARGE OF PUBLIC RELATIONS
AND WILL GIVE US HIS FULL ASSISTANCE...

OK, LET'S START
RIGHT AWAY.

SCENE 2, SHOT 1: THE YOUNG ROOKIE
MOVES INTO THE DORMITORY.

SCENE 2, SHOT 3: THE YOUNG ROOKIE
VISITS THE ARMY MEDICAL FACILITIES.

SCENE 5, SHOT 2: THE YOUNG ROOKIE LEARNS
HOW TO USE A KALASHNIKOV.

SMILE,
YOU'RE ON
CAMERA!

SMILE,
YOU'RE IN
MY SIGHTS!

COLONEL SHAPUR IS ASKING
IF YOU'RE A TRAINED WAR
PHOTOGRAPHER.

NOT REALLY. I'M A
TRAINED CHILDREN'S-BOOK
ILLUSTRATOR...

SCENE 9. EXTERIOR. DAY: THE SOLDIERS ARE DOING PHYSICAL TRAINING...

DO YOU THINK THIS SHOT'S GOING TO LOOK COOL?

KINDA CONCEPTUAL, Y'KNOW.

CLICK

THE AMERICANS ARE SO STUPID, THOUGH...

AFTER 1986, THEY ARMED THE MUJAHIDEEN TO FIGHT AGAINST THE RUSSIANS...

CLICK

THEN IN THE NINETIES, THEY SUPPORTED THE TALIBAN, WHO WERE FIGHTING THE MUJAHIDEEN...

CLICK

AND NOW THEY'RE TRAINING AND FUNDING A WHOLE ARMY TO FIGHT THE TALIBAN...

CLICK

YEAH, THEY SPEND THEIR TIME CREATING NEW ENEMIES. IT'S THEIR LITTLE GAME...

WHO KNOWS? IN THE 2010s, THEY MIGHT CREATE AND ARM A NEW FORCE TO FIGHT THE AFGHAN ARMY...

CLICK

WELL... AS LONG AS THEY GET US TO DO THEIR RECRUITMENT CAMPAIGN!

HA HA!

HA HA!

FEELS GOOD TO START THE DAY WITH A DASH OF CYNICISM...

CLICK

I SAY WE GIVE UP ON THIS DUMB SHOT...

OOOF ...

IN THE AFTERNOON, WE FOLLOW SEVERAL ANA BATTALIONS SIMULATING
MILITARY MANEUVERS IN THE HILLS BEHIND KMTC.

THAT NIGHT, AT THE GUESTHOUSE...

WE WENT THROUGH A VALLEY FILLED WITH THE REMAINS OF SOVIET TANKS. I FELT LIKE I WAS WANDERING DOWN THE CORRIDORS OF HISTORY...

GETTING PRESIDENTS ELECTED ISN'T LAURIE WHITE'S ONLY TALENT. SHE ALSO MAKES A MEAN BLOODY MARY.

WHEN I THINK THAT IT WAS HARDER TO FIND TABASCO THAN VODKA...

KABUL, LAND OF CONTRASTS...

SANTÉ!

CHEERS!

WELL, SOMEONE PROPOSED TO ME TODAY!

YEAH? WHO?

A WARLORD I'M GIVING POLITICAL COMMUNICATION LESSONS TO. THE PEOPLE OF HIS PROVINCE SEE HIM AS THE REINCARNATION OF A PROPHET!

PICTURE ME ENDING MY DAYS IN SOME LOST AFGHAN VALLEY, WIPING THE ASSES OF A WARLORD'S BRATS?

AH! THE PERFECT PUNISHMENT FOR THE WOMAN WHO GOT GEORGE BUSH ELECTED...

HA HA! SMARTASS!

AND HE'S NOT THE WORST. THE OTHER CANDIDATES INCLUDE DRUG TRAFFICKERS AND FORMER TALIBAN...

IN ALL, 300 CANDIDATES HAVE BLOOD ON THEIR HANDS.

YET ONLY 25 OF THEM WERE DECLARED INELIGIBLE BY THE JEMB*.

WHY'S THAT?

*U.N. JOINT ELECTORAL MONITORING BODY.

BECAUSE THE JEMB REALIZES THAT THESE PEOPLE ARE POTENTIALLY DANGEROUS. IF THEY DON'T WIN POWER AT THE POLLS, THEY'LL TAKE IT BY FORCE...

O AFGHANS! REBUILD YOUR COUNTRY BY ELECTING THE ONES WHO DESTROYED IT!

?

WHAT'S THIS?

A PROTOTYPE OF THE VOTING SLIP. SINCE MOST VOTERS ARE ILLITERATE, THEY HAVE TO DRAW AN X NEXT TO THEIR CANDIDATE'S SYMBOL.

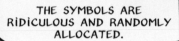

THE SYMBOLS ARE RIDICULOUS AND RANDOMLY ALLOCATED.

YES, I HAVE TO TEACH THE CANDIDATES HOW TO "SELL" THEMSELVES USING DUMB SYMBOLS LIKE PIPELINES, PUMPKINS AND POTATO MASHERS!

HUH... IN FRANCE, ONE OF OUR PRESIDENTS GOT IN USING AN APPLE TREE...

YEAH, IN THE STATES WE ALSO VOTE FOR AN ELEPHANT OR A DONKEY EVERY FOUR YEARS...

BUT STILL, VOTING FOR A POTATO MASHER!

SQUELCH!

SAY NO TO VAGUE POLITICAL SPEECHS! NO TO NON-TRANSPARENCY!

SAY YES TO CLEAR RHETORIC AND A LONG-TERM VISION FOR THE COUNTRY!

VOTE FOR:

GLASSES IN A CIRCLE.

IN THE QUR'ĀN, AS IN OUR COUNTRY'S CONSTITUTION, WOMEN PLAY A PROMINENT ROLE.

FOR GREATER FREEDOM AND TRUE ACTION TO BENEFIT AFGHAN WOMEN...

...VOTE FOR:

THREE TANKS IN A SQUARE.

THE TALIBAN STOOD FOR ORDER AND JUSTICE IN OUR COUNTRY...

IF YOU'RE FED UP WITH THE GENERAL CHAOS AND WANT A RETURN TO STRONG LEADERSHIP...

...VOTE FOR:

TWO CARE BEARS IN A SQUARE.

TODAY, KABULI!

AGAIN?

IT'S AN ASSAULT ON GOOD TASTE!

MAYBE AL-QAEDA'S PAYING THE COOK TO POISON US?

SALÂM, FRIENDS!

HEY, HARUN! TO WHAT DO WE OWE THE PLEASURE?

HAVE YOU GOT THE OFFICE CAMERA?

YES.

I NEED A PHOTO OF A ROSE FROM THE GARDEN.

ENJOY!

DAMN! YOUR ROSE BUSHES ARE IN THE SHADE!

WELL, WE'LL JUST CUT ONE AND TAKE A PICTURE IN THE SUN.

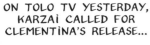

ON TOLO TV YESTERDAY, KARZAI CALLED FOR CLEMENTINA'S RELEASE...

...AND ENDED HIS SPEECH WITH "FREE CLEMENTINA, THE ROSE OF AFGHANISTA."

MEH, THE PETALS ARE A BIT WITHERED...

THE CARE NGO – WHERE CLEMENTINA WORKS – ASKED US TO DESIGN A STICKER.

LET'S TAKE ANOTHER!

NWILD 10 JUIN 2007

IN THE CENTRE OF THE STICKER WILL BE A ROSE WITH KARZAI'S WORDS AROUND IT, IN DARI AND PASHTO.

IT'LL BE SENT OUT ALL OVER THE COUNTRY.

OH YUCK! THE STEM'S ALL BROKEN...

IT'S FUNNY TO SEE HOW A SIMPLE KIDNAPPING GETS THE INTERNATIONAL COMMUNITY SO AGITATED...

LOTS OF AFGHANS GET ABDUCTED EVERY WEEK AND NO ONE TALKS ABOUT IT...

ONE OF MY COUSINS WAS KIDNAPPED BY A TRIBAL CHIEF FROM A NEIGHBORING VALLEY...

NO, THE PISTILS ARE MILDEWY!

THE TRIBAL CHIEF WANTED TO PUT LOTS OF PRESSURE ON MY COUSIN'S FATHER FOR HIM TO SETTLE A PETTY LAND SQUABBLE.

BUT THE TWO MEN, BOTH STUBBORN, NEVER CAME TO AN AGREEMENT...

CLICK

SO MY COUSIN STAYED WITH THE TRIBAL CHIEF...

...MARRIED HIS DAUGHTER, AND NOW HAS TWO CHILDREN WITH HIM.

YES! *THAT'S OUR* CLEMENTINA!

KHUB AST!

THERE'S A CAR LEAVING FOR THE OFFICE. YOU COMING?

MORE AND MORE ELECTION POSTERS ARE GOING UP. IF THEY KEEP ON, THE STREETS WILL BE UNRECOGNIZABLE SOON...

YOU'RE SPOILED FOR CHOICE. ANY IDEA WHO YOU'LL VOTE FOR?

VOTE FOR ME!

AH, GOOD OLD CHIJAN! ARE YOU RUNNING? DOESN'T BEING A FORMER KGB TORTURER MAKE YOU INELIGIBLE?

YOU CAN TALK! I'M NOT THE ONE WHO DEFORESTED OUR LAND AND SOLD THE TIMBER TO PAKISTAN DURING THE WAR!

NO, OF COURSE NOT! YOU WERE TOO BUSY TORTURING MAOIST DISSIDENTS FROM HAZARAJAT!

SHIT! WHO STUCK ME UP ABOVE THESE TWO PARWAN SISSIES?

SHUT UP, YOU EX-TALIBAN!

WHAT DO YOU MEAN, "EX"? I'M STILL A TALIBAN! IF THERE WAS A STREET LIGHT HERE, I'D STRING YOU UP LIKE NAJIBULLAH!

ALL THIS VIOLENCE DISGUSTS ME. MORE THAN EVER, I FEEL THAT WOMEN ARE THIS LAND'S FUTURE.

A WOMAN'S PLACE IS NO LONGER AT THE OVEN!

AT THE OVEN? NO! MORE LIKE *IN* THE OVEN!

HEY, TALIBAN, DID YOU FORGET YOUR MOTHER'S A WOMAN?

I NEVER FORGET! I DON'T SPEND MY TIME SMOKING OPIUM!

I DON'T SMOKE OPIUM, I SELL IT! ER... WHOOPS!

DRUG TRAFFICKERS PUT OUR COUNTRY TO SHAME!

AT LEAST I GIVE WORK TO THE PEASANTS!

NO, YOU EXPLOIT THEM. IT'S DESPICABLE!

IS JOAN OF ARC GONNA SHUT UP?!

HEY, BEARDY! LEARN TO READ AND GET YOURSELF A GUIDE ON SOCIAL ETIQUETTE!

BAMIYAN PEASANT!

ORGAN-PEDDLE

CHEAP WHORE!

NEO-DICK!

KREMLIN STOOGE!

CHIL EXPLO

BANDIT!

TWO-BIT MONARCHIST!

RXISF-VINIST!

OPIUM-EATER!

TH AMERICAN LAPDOG!

WAHHA-BITE ME!

PAKISTANI PUPPET!

PANJSHIR RASCAL!

OPIUM DEALER!

VILLAIN!

CROOK!

SO, WILL YOU CHOOSE "THREE TANKS IN A SQUARE," "A PUMPKIN IN A CIRCLE," OR "TWO CEDARS IN A SQUARE"?

LOOKING AT THAT LOT, I THINK I'LL CHOOSE TWO ASPIRINS IN A GLASS OF WATER!

THE MAN WHO ABDUCTED CLEMENTINA IS CALLING HIMSELF "TIMUR SHAH," AFTER AN OLD AFGHAN KING.

(HE WISHES TO REMAIN ANONYMOUS).

HE'S USING HIS HOSTAGE TO PRESSURE THE AFGHAN GOVERNMENT INTO FREEING HIS MOTHER.

TIMUR'S MOTHER IS IN PRISON FOR HELPING HER SON ESCAPE FROM PRISON LAST YEAR...

THIS ABDUCTION IS YET ANOTHER CHAPTER IN AN ACTION-PACKED AFGHAN SAGA.

THE AFGHAN WIDOWS CLEMENTINA WORKED WITH ARE STAGING A DEMONSTRATION TODAY TO DEMAND HER RELEASE...

WE'RE GONNA BE LATE AT KMTC...

LATER...

WE'LL GO SET UP THE COMPUTER-ROOM SCENE.

CALL ME WHEN YOU'RE READY. I'LL SIT DOWN SOMEWHERE AND START TOUCHING UP YESTERDAY'S PHOTOS.

*FAMOUS FRENCH SINGER/SONGWRITER.

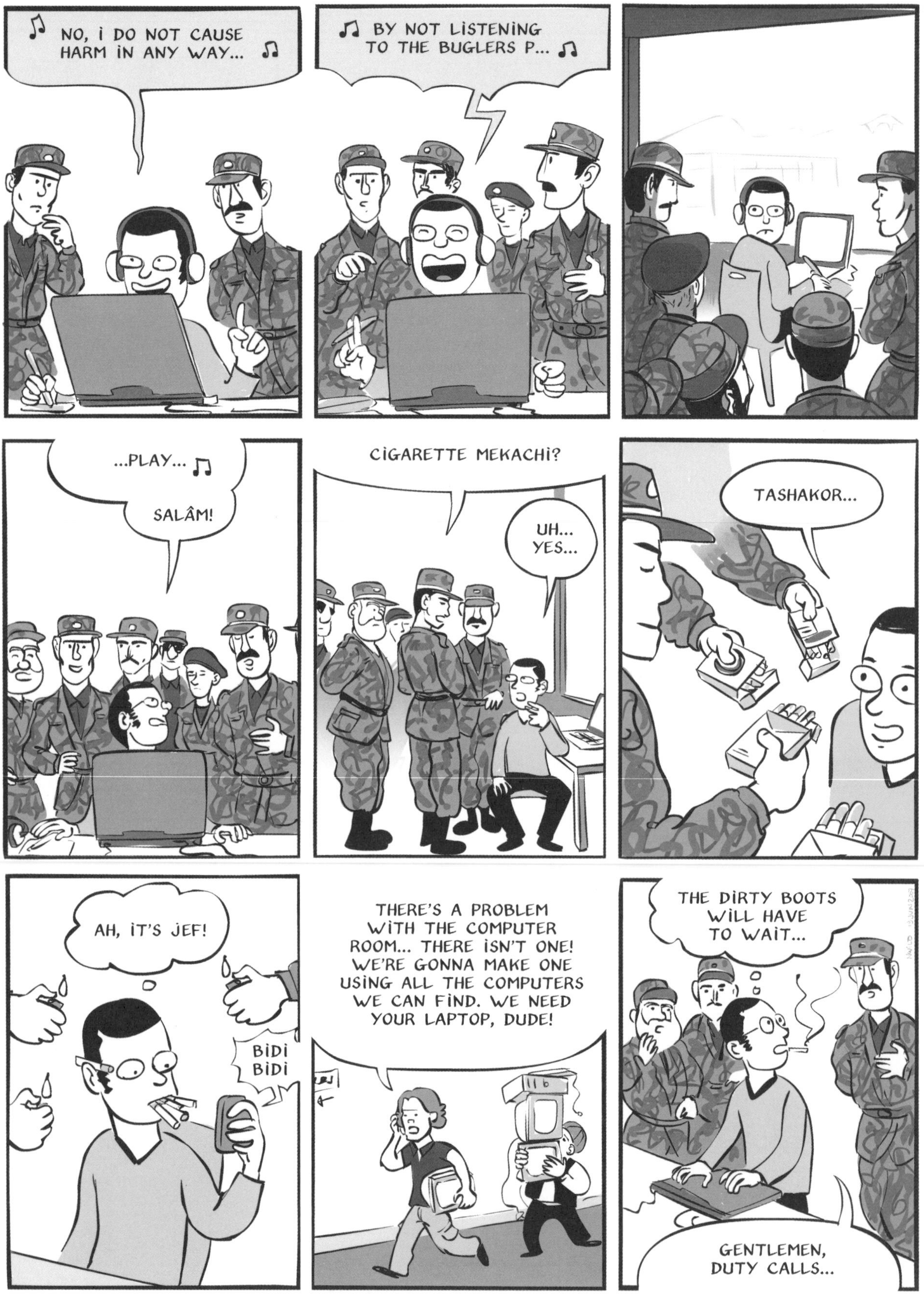
♫ NO, I DO NOT CAUSE HARM IN ANY WAY... ♫
♫ BY NOT LISTENING TO THE BUGLERS P... ♫
...PLAY... ♫
SALÂM!
CIGARETTE MEKACHI?
UH... YES...
TASHAKOR...
AH, IT'S JEF!
BIDI BIDI
THERE'S A PROBLEM WITH THE COMPUTER ROOM... THERE ISN'T ONE! WE'RE GONNA MAKE ONE USING ALL THE COMPUTERS WE CAN FIND. WE NEED YOUR LAPTOP, DUDE!
THE DIRTY BOOTS WILL HAVE TO WAIT...
GENTLEMEN, DUTY CALLS...

THE KMTC CANTEEN FEEDS MORE THAN 8,000 SOLDIERS A DAY...

SO QUANTITY PREVAILS OVER QUALITY...

DRY RICE

MUTTON FAT

ROTTEN BANANA

ONION SALAD (NO DRESSING)

STILL, ONE OF THE POSTERS CLAIMS THAT THE ARMY WILL GIVE YOU "THREE HOT MEALS A DAY"...

SHIT! IT'S THE SAME THING AS YESTERDAY!

IT'S LIKE THEY WANT 'EM TO DESERT!

THEY SAY FRENCH SOLDIERS GET CHEESE PLATTERS, COLD MEATS, AND ROSÉ WINE...

YEAH? WHY DID I EVER FAKE BEING NUTS TO GET OUT OF MILITARY SERVICE?

FAKE "FIT FOR SERVICE" NEXT TIME!

SCENE 59. EXTERIOR. DAY: A BATTALION OF SOLDIERS MARCHES TOWARD THE CAMERA.

POOR GUYS. TO THINK THAT SOME OF THEM WILL BE SENT TO THE FRONT TO FIGHT THE TALIBAN...

ZOOM.

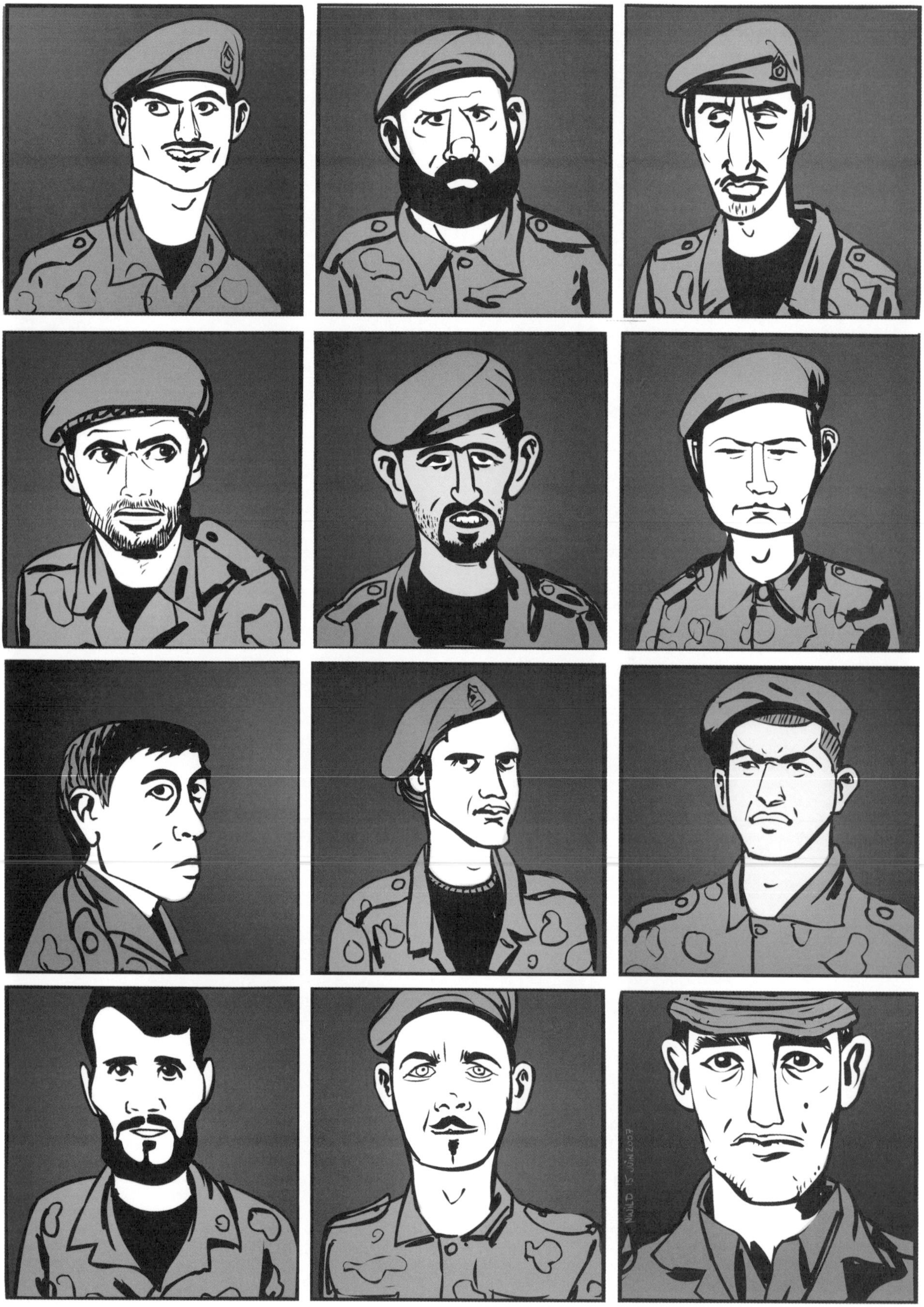

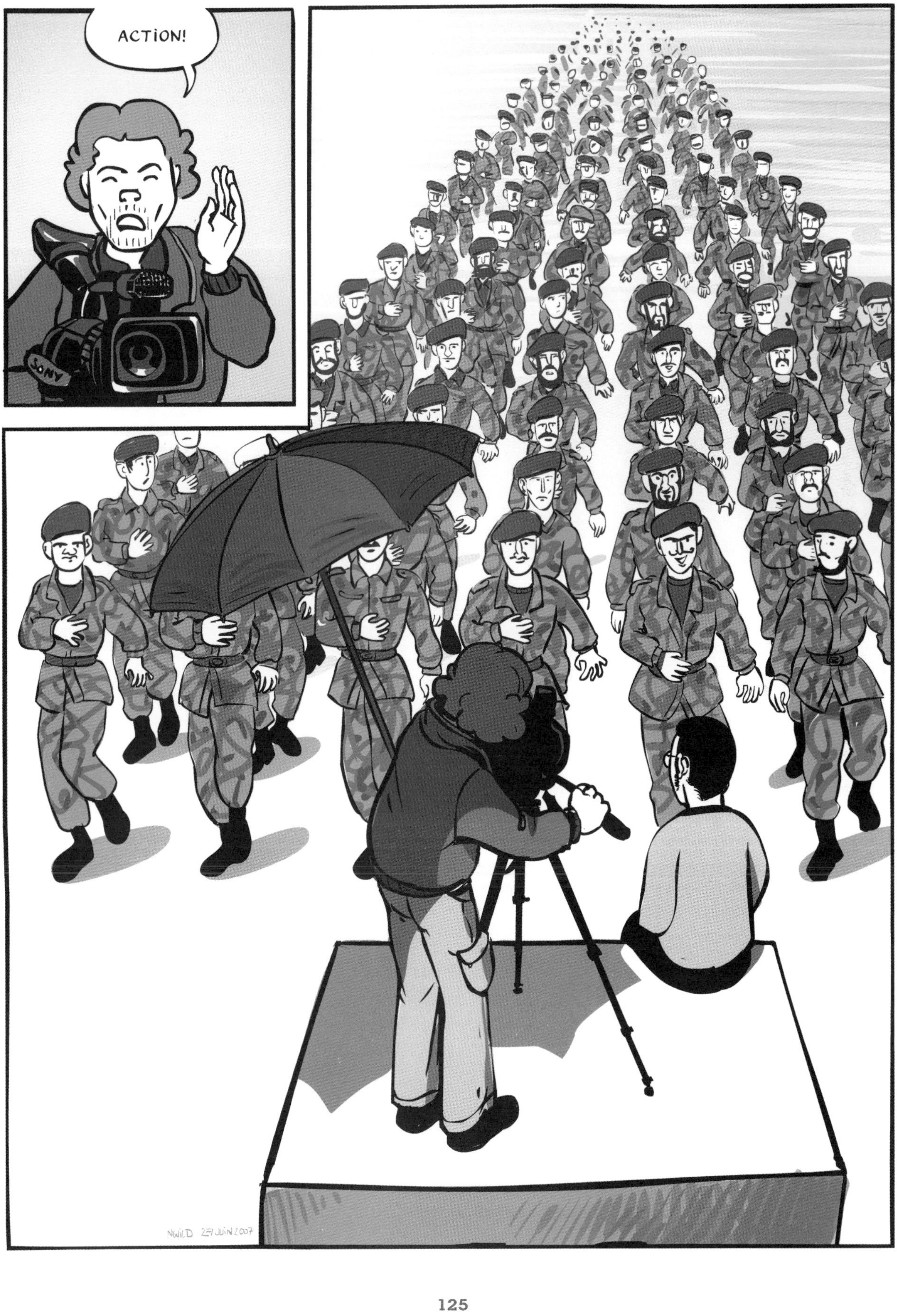
ACTION!

THAT EVENING...

WE DID FIFTEEN TAKES OF THE MARCHING ARMY SHOT!

AND COULDN'T EVEN GET TWO SOLDIERS TO WALK IN SYNC.

AS WE LOOKED THROUGH THE RUSHES LATER, JEF REALIZED THAT THE ONLY GOOD SHOT HAD A SOLDIER WAVING AT THE CAMERA IN IT. HE WAS FURIOUS.

SEEN THIS? THERE'S AN AD FOR A BOSNIAN RESTAURANT IN *AFGHAN SCENE*.

"THE BEST SCHNITZEL IN KABUL SINCE 2004."

WE'RE NOT ALLOWED TO LEAVE THE HOUSE AFTER CURFEW.

IT'S CRAZY, THE RESTAURANT'S RIGHT NEXT DOOR AND WE'VE NEVER BEEN.

WE'RE NOT. ALLOWED. TO LEAVE. THE HOUSE. AFTER CURFEW.

"ASK FOR OUR WINE LIST..."

COULD WE HAVE THE WINE LIST, PLEASE?

WE SHOULDN'T BE HERE.

THERE ARE TWO...

ER, NO. TWO WINES...

TWO LISTS?

WHICH TWO?

ONE WITH A KANGAROO ON THE LABEL, AND ONE WITH SPANISH WRITING...

RIGHT! GIVE US A BOTTLE OF YOUR MOST EXPENSIVE! MY TREAT!

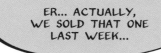

ER... ACTUALLY, WE SOLD THAT ONE LAST WEEK...

THERE'S ONLY THE CHEAPER ONE, BUT IT DOES HAVE A KANGAROO!

AHEM.

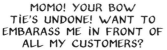

MOMO! YOUR BOW TIE'S UNDONE! WANT TO EMBARASS ME IN FRONT OF ALL MY CUSTOMERS?

SINCE THE KIDNAPPINGS STARTED UP AGAIN IN THE NEIGHBORHOOD, NO ONE COMES ANYMORE...

YOU'RE OUR FIRST CUSTOMERS IN TWO WEEKS.

THE OTHER WAITERS AND THE CHEF HAVE ALL LEFT...

IF YOU FANCY A CHANGE OF SCENE, THE AFGHAN ARMY'S RECRUITING...

NO, I'M STAYING!

FOR HER... ♥

MOMO, OFFER THOSE TWO TURKISH DIGNITARIES A GLASS OF SUNQUICK ON THE HOUSE.

GO TO THE BAR FOR A DRINK, THEN EAT AT HOME. OUR FRIDGES ARE EMPTY...

WOW! SUNQUICK! HAVEN'T HAD IT SINCE I WAS TEN...

MEANWHILE, AT THE TAIMANI GUESTHOUSE...

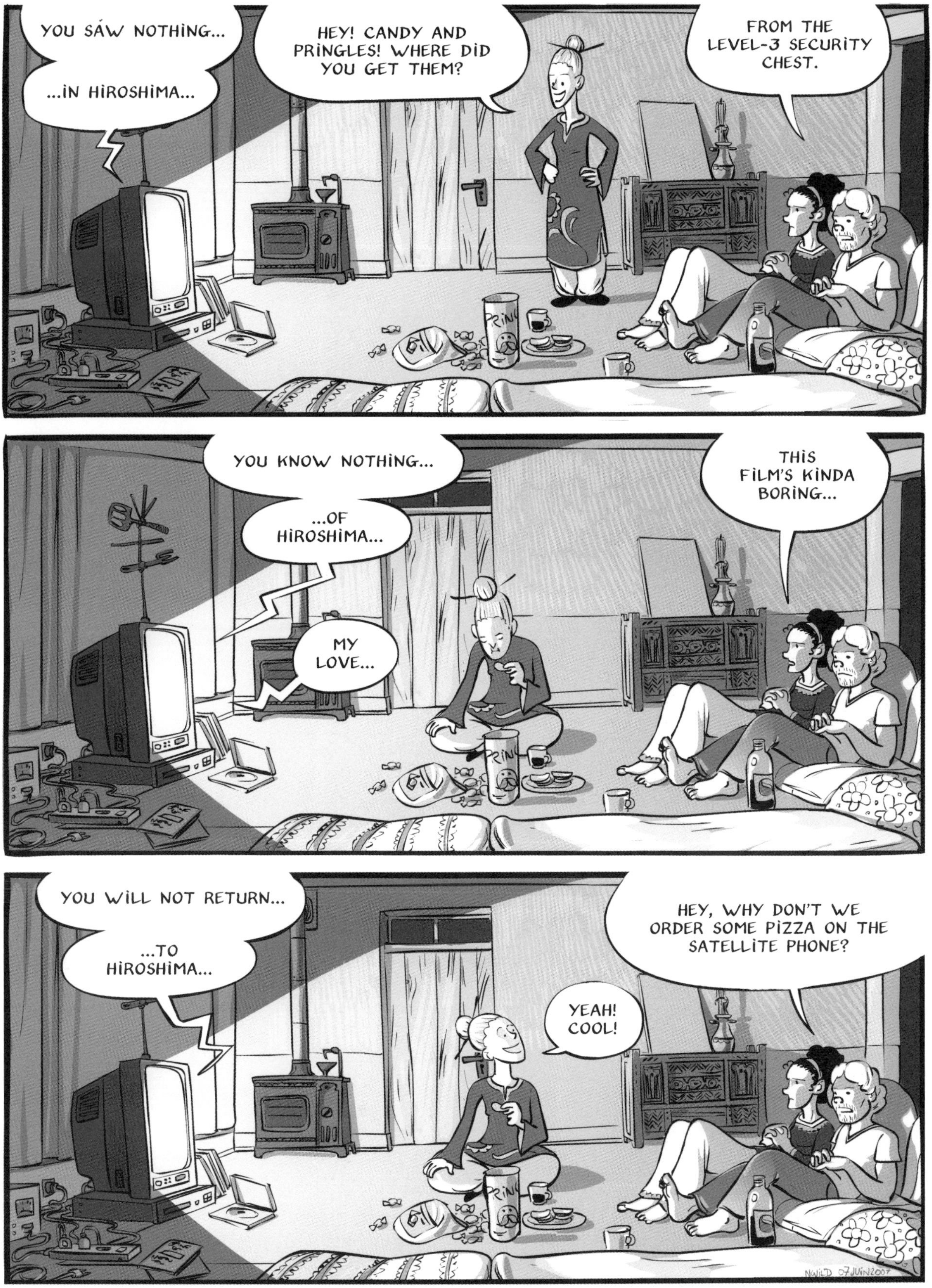
YOU SAW NOTHING...
...IN HIROSHIMA...
HEY! CANDY AND PRINGLES! WHERE DID YOU GET THEM?
FROM THE LEVEL-3 SECURITY CHEST.
YOU KNOW NOTHING...
...OF HIROSHIMA...
MY LOVE...
THIS FILM'S KINDA BORING...
YOU WILL NOT RETURN...
...TO HIROSHIMA...
YEAH! COOL!
HEY, WHY DON'T WE ORDER SOME PIZZA ON THE SATELLITE PHONE?
NWILD 07JUIN2007

THAT WASN'T SUNQUICK!

RIGHT, IF WE CALL TO SAY WE'RE LOST, THEY'LL KNOW WE WERE OUT AFTER CURFEW.

NEVER MIND THAT. GIVE ME YOUR PHONE. MINE'S DEAD...

UH... SO'S MINE.

THE CAR! IT'S REVERSING TOWARDS US!

WE'RE GONNA BE ABDUCTED...

¡¡¡

GULP

AHEM!

EDOUARD?

I DON'T EVEN WANNA KNOW WHY YOU'RE INFRINGING ON THE MOST BASIC OF SECURITY RULES. YOU'VE GOT THREE SECONDS TO GO HOME. AND I WANNA SEE YOU TWO IN MY OFFICE FIRST THING IN THE MORNING...

THAT SUCKS! I'D RATHER BE KIDNAPPED THAN BUMP INTO HIM!

WE SHOULD'VE ASKED HIM FOR A LIFT BACK.

OH, IT'S YOU... I HEARD A CAR. I THOUGHT IT WAS THE PIZZA DELIVERY GUY.

LÉA?

FOLLOWING THE CONSERVATIVE MAHMOUD AHMADINEJAD'S ELECTION VICTORY IN IRAN, GEORGE BUSH HAS DECIDED TO INVADE THE COUNTRY.

THE INVASION WAS LAUNCHED FROM TWO COUNTRIES ALREADY OCCUPIED BY THE U.S. ARMY.

WE COULDNA RESPONDED SO QUICK WITHOUT THE AFGHAN ARMY'S HELP...

THE U.S. ARMY TRAINED, FUNDED AND ARMED THE AFGHAN ARMY.

A GREAT EXAMPLE OF AFGHAN-AMERICAN COOPERATION.

TELL ME, CORPORAL AHMAD, HOW AND WHY DID YOU END UP JOINING THE RANKS OF THE AFGHAN ARMY?

IT WAS THANKS TO A PROPAGANDA POSTER THEY STUCK UP IN MY NEIGHBORHOOD...

THE PHOTOS WERE SO COOL AND WELL-PHOTOSHOPPED THAT I RAN STRAIGHT OFF TO ENLIST...

ENROLL AFGHAN ARMY

A
A

N

. 3 HOT MEALS A DAY!!!

LET'S MEET ONE OF THE YOUNG GRAPHIC DESIGNERS WHO WORKED ON THE POSTER IN QUESTION.

inTOX NEWS channel

HELLO ♫

FREE CLEMENTINA

MR. NICOLAS, HOW DOES IT FEEL TO BE RESPONSIBLE FOR THIS UNJUST AND BLOODY INVASION WAR?

inTOX NEWS channel

LIVE FROM KABUL

OH, I'M SO FLATTERED... DON'T MAKE ME BLUSH...

WAAAAHHH!!!

DRIP

MUST EMPTY THAT BUCKET ONE DAY...

HAVE YOU SEEN *KABUL WEEKLY* TODAY?

UH...

PAGE TWO: 100 AFGHAN SOLDIERS DESERT IN LOGAR PROVINCE. WHY? BECAUSE THEY DIDN'T GET PAID FOR THREE MONTHS! MEANWHILE, AL-QAEDA IS HIRING AND PAYING TWICE AS MUCH! WHAT DO YOU THINK?

DUNNO. MAYBE IF WE WERE DOING AL-QAEDA'S CAMPAIGNS, THEY'D PAY *US* BETTER...

HA HA

STOP MESSING AROUND! LOOK AT THE POSTER YOU'VE JUST FINISHED!

THIS SOLDIER'S JUST GOT HIS SALARY: "JOIN THE ARMY, IT'S A WELL-PAID JOB, GUARANTEED"!

WE LIED! WE'RE SPREADING FALSE INFORMATION!

IT'S OUTRAGEOUS!

OUT-RA-GEOUS!

ALL OF IT MIGHT BE BULLSHIT! TAKE THIS IMAGE OF A COMPUTER LESSON... HOW DO WE KNOW IT ISN'T FAKE? MAYBE THAT COMPUTER ROOM DOESN'T EVEN EXIST!

HAVE YOU SEEN *KABUL WEEKLY* TODAY?

UH...

THERE'S BEEN AN ATTACK ON JALALABAD ROAD.

A BIKE-BOMB WAS DRIVEN AT A SWEDISH ARMY VEHICLE. THE DRIVER MANAGED TO AVOID THE BIKE, BUT IT ENDED UP CRASHING INTO A TAXI FULL OF AFGHANS. SEVEN INJURED, THEY SAY.

HEY! IT'S ONE OF MY TWO FAVORITE ILLUSTRATORS. HAVE YOU SEEN *KABUL WEEKLY* TODAY?

I THINK I'M GONNA SUBSCRIBE...

THE TRANSPORT MINISTER HAS JUST BANNED AZERBAIJAN AIRLINES FROM LANDING IN KABUL. YOUR RETURN TICKET'S WITH THEM, ISN'T IT?

UMM...

I CAN'T TAKE IT! I WANNA GO BACK TO FRANCE!

WHAT, YOU'RE FEELING BLUE? I THINK I STILL HAVE A BOTTLE OF RIESLING AT HOME. WHAT ARE YOU UP TO TONIGHT?

I CAN'T TAKE IT! I WANNA GO BACK HOME!

135

SO, TOMORROW YOU'RE OFF ON HOLIDAY. HAPPY?

OH YES!

FLYING BACK VIA BAKU?

OH NO!

FOR SOME OBSCURE REASON, AZERBAIJAN AIRLINES HAS SUSPENDED ALL ITS FLIGHTS TO KABUL. I HAD TO BUY A LAST-MINUTE TICKET...

LEMME SEE!

KABUL-DUBAI, DUBAI-MOSCOW, MOSCOW-PARIS! LOOKS LIKE YOU WON A ROUND-THE-WORLD JAUNT ON A TV GAME SHOW!

YEAH! I'LL BE ABLE TO COMPARE SWISS CHOCOLATE PRICES IN DUTY-FREE SHOPS AT FOUR DIFFERENT AIRPORTS!

LÉA? THE "FREE CLEMENTINA, ROSE OF AFGHANISTAN" STICKERS ARE HERE.

OH, THANKS, TOUARELAI!

THE FAMOUS STICKER THAT COST ME THREE ROSE BUSHES!

THERE'S PLENTY MORE ROSES ON THE BUSH! HA HA!

RIGHT, LET'S BRIGHTEN UP OUR WORKPLACE!

SPLAT

BIDI BIDI

HELLO? VALENTIN?

OH MY GOD!

WHAT HAPPENED?

IT'S CLEMENTINA...

SHE... SHE...

SHE... SHE?

SHE'S BEEN RELEASED!

OH WOW! WAS IT BECAUSE OF MY STICKER?

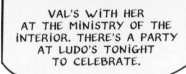

VAL'S WITH HER AT THE MINISTRY OF THE INTERIOR. THERE'S A PARTY AT LUDO'S TONIGHT TO CELEBRATE.

THE CURFEW'S BEEN EXTENDED TILL 3 AM FOR THE OCCASION! YAY!

A PARTY?

UH, LÉA?

WHAT DO WE DO WITH ALL THESE STICKERS?

♫ SEX BOMB ♫ SEX BOMB ♫

OH!

YOU'RE MY SEX B

HEY! HI, LUDO!

OH, HEY NICOLAS! YOU SHOULD DITCH THE SHIRT! GONNA GET HOT IN HERE, MAN!

YOU THINK SO?

OMB ♫ .. .. YOU

SKRITCH

CAN GIVE IT

HEEHEE LUDO! ♥

YEAH, I THINK SO.

HERE.

TO ME WHEN

HI THERE, BUDDY!

TRISTAN? YOU LOOK MERRY!

I'M DRUNK!

I NEED TO

YOU'RE AN OKAY GUY. HANG ON, WAIT... L-LEMME TELL YOU... YOU, YOU...

YOU'RE AN O-OKAY GUY.

COME ALONG

I KNOW I... I KNOW I'M A PAIN IN THE ASS SOMETIMES...

OH, NO...

YEAH, I CAN BE...

I CAN, I KNOW!

NWILD 15 JUIN 2007

♪♫ AND BABY

BUT SOMETIMES I'M A PAIN, HUH? BUT YOU... YOU'RE AN OKAY G-GUY.

YOU CAN TURN

YEEAAH! C'MON NICO, LET'S GO BOOGIE!

HI, MAUD!

ME ON ♪♫♫

COME ON! ALL OF ZENDAGUI WITH ME! LET'S DANCE IN A BIG CIRCLE!

VAL!

SEX BOMB ♫ SEX BOMB

LET'S GO OUT IN THE MIDDLE SO EVERYONE CAN SEE US!

YOU'RE MY SEX BOMB ♫

YEEHAA!!!

YO!

♫♪ AND BABY

HEY, DUDE! BET YOU CAN'T DOWN THIS IN ONE!

YOU INSULT ME, DEAR WATSON!

YOU CAN TURN

BOTTOMS UP!

ME ON ♪♫♫

DRINK IT DOWN! HA HA!

139

CAN I HAVE A BOTTLE OF ASPIRIN, PLEASE, AND THREE LITERS OF WATER?

THE WORST HANGOVER IN MY LIFE, AND ALL BECAUSE OF CLEMENTINA...

DO YOU GET SICK ON PLANES?

COULD YOU OPEN THE WINDOW? I THINK I'M GOING TO VOMIT...

USE THIS INSTEAD.

BARFFF

MIKE, MY NEIGHBOR ON THE PLANE, IS AN AMERICAN WHO BUILT SCHOOLS IN KANDAHAR. HE'S BEEN THROUGH LOTS OF CRAZY STUFF, LIKE HE ONCE AVOIDED A SUICIDE ATTACK.

JEALOUS, I SHOWED HIM YASSIN & KAKA RAOUF TO TURN THE CONVERSATION ONTO ME. HE LOVED IT.

NOT BAD...

LADIES AND GENTLEMEN, WE WILL SOON BE LANDING IN DUBAI...

140

MY FLIGHT TO MOSCOW IS IN EIGHT HOURS. I CAN BEGIN MY RESEARCH ON SWISS CHOCOLATE PRICES IN DUTY-FREE SHOPS.

BAGS

OR YOU CAN COME TO MY PLACE FOR A DRINK.

OK.

IN JUST TEN YEARS, DUBAI'S BECOME THE NEW YORK OF THE MIDDLE EAST.

TAXI ▼ LIMO ▶

ONE AMBITIOUS ARCHITECTURAL DESIGN SHOOTS UP AFTER ANOTHER. ON YOUR LEFT IS AN INDOOR SKI SLOPE.

ON THE COAST, THEY'VE BUILT ARCHIPELAGOS SHAPED LIKE PALM TREES AND A WORLD MAP.

THIS YEAR, THEY STARTED BUILDING THE WORLD'S TALLEST TOWER: 828 METERS!!

OVER TWICE THE HEIGHT OF THE EMPIRE STATE BUILDING.

TA-DA! WELCOME TO MY PLACE!

OH DAMN, I FORGOT TO GRAB MY MAIL. YOU GO IN, I WON'T BE LONG...

OK.

OH!

SURPRR...

...RISE!!!

WELCOME BA[CK]

UH, ACTUALLY I'M A FRIEND OF MIKE'S...

OH!

HOLY COW!

SURPRISE!!!

WE SAT NEXT TO EACH OTHER ON THE PLANE...

...AND SINCE I HAD AN EIGHT-HOUR WAIT...

MIKEY, GIMME A HUG!

JIM HAD A SPARE SET OF KEYS! THAT'S HOW WE GOT IN!

WONDERFUL SURPRISE!

...FOR MY MOSCOW FLIGHT...

WELL...

YOU DID LOSE WEIGHT IN AFGHANISTAN!

I'M SO GLAD!

PLEASE DON'T GO BACK THERE!

UH... I'LL BRING THE BAGS IN, OK?

DO YOU HAVE PHOTOS OF TORA BORA?

PLENTY!

DO WOMEN STILL WEAR BURQAS IN KANDAHAR?

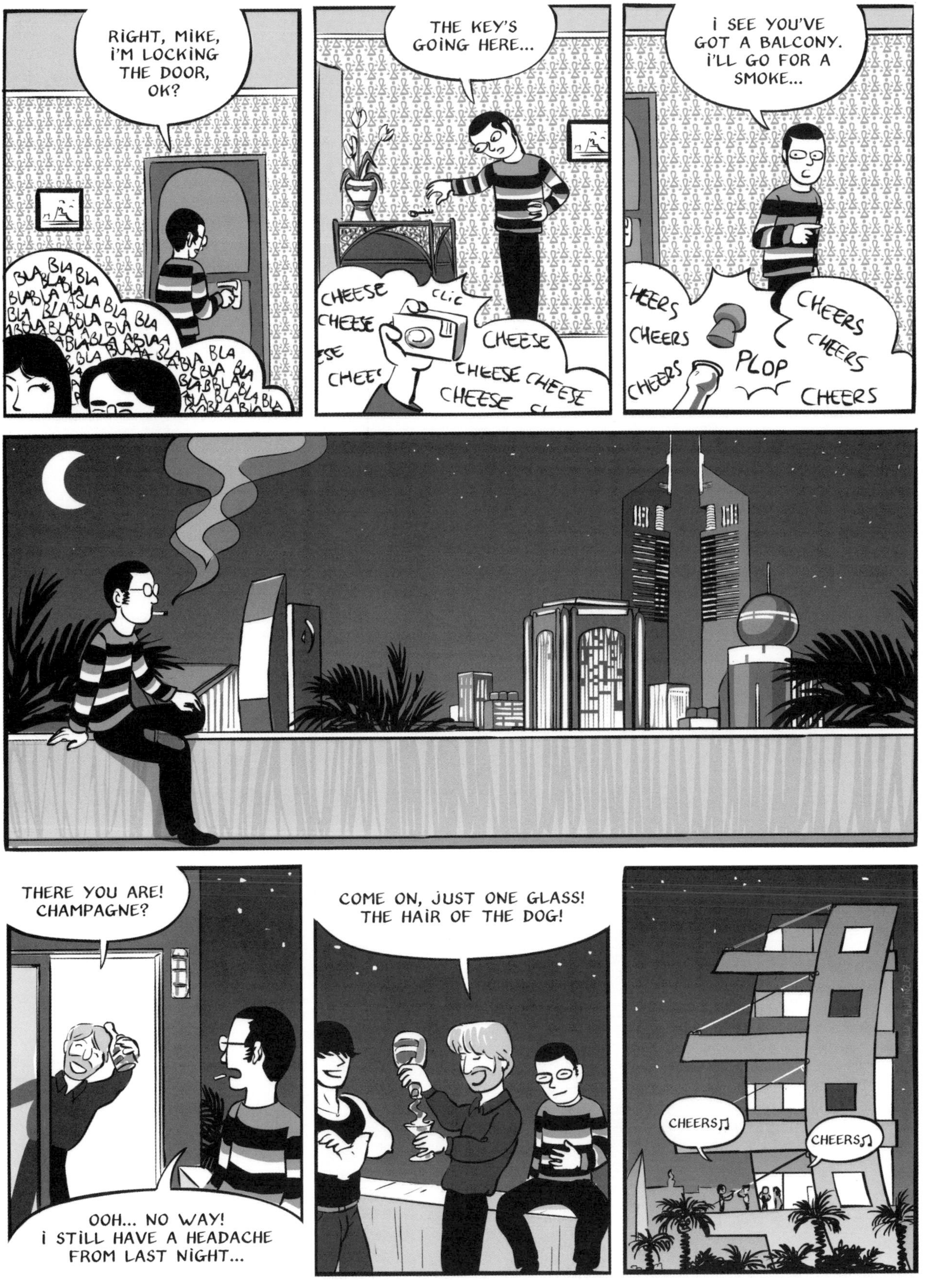
RIGHT, MIKE, I'M LOCKING THE DOOR, OK?
THE KEY'S GOING HERE...
CLIC
I SEE YOU'VE GOT A BALCONY. I'LL GO FOR A SMOKE...
PLOP
THERE YOU ARE! CHAMPAGNE?
OOH... NO WAY! I STILL HAVE A HEADACHE FROM LAST NIGHT...
COME ON, JUST ONE GLASS! THE HAIR OF THE DOG!
CHEERS♫
CHEERS♫

SIR? WE'VE ARRIVED... SIR?

HUH? NOT GOING TO WORK... SICK...

SIR, WE'VE ARRIVED IN MOSCOW.

WHAT?

BOOZE ON BOOZE! IT'S ALL VERY WOOZY...

OH, A SOUVENIR SHOP SELLING SOVIET PROPAGANDA POSTERS FROM THE 1930S...

HOW MUCH FOR THE DEATH TO CAPITALISM POSTER?

CAN I PAY IN DOLLARS?

350 ROUBLES.

OF COURSE.

SEVERAL HOURS LATER...

MÉNILMONTANT, PARIS...

YOO-HOO! I'M HOME!

WAHOO! THAT'S MY 15TH COMIC BOOK DONE!

JUST GOTTA BURN IT ONTO A DVD AND ZAP IT OFF TO MY PUBLISHER...

I BROUGHT YOU A SOVIET POSTER.

COOL. I'M CHATTING WITH CAPUCINE.

BE WITH YOU IN FIVE...

THERE'S BEER IN THE FRIDGE...

YUCK! I'M THROUGH WITH ALCOHOL!

DID YOU CONVERT TO ISLAM?

HAHA. AND HERE'S BOULET, THE WITTIEST GUY IN THE GALAXY!

CAPUCINE HAS POKED YOU!

LOL!

SNORE.

ONE HOUR LATER...

SO, YOU GOING BACK TO AFGHANISTAN?

ONLY AFTER MY SIESTA...

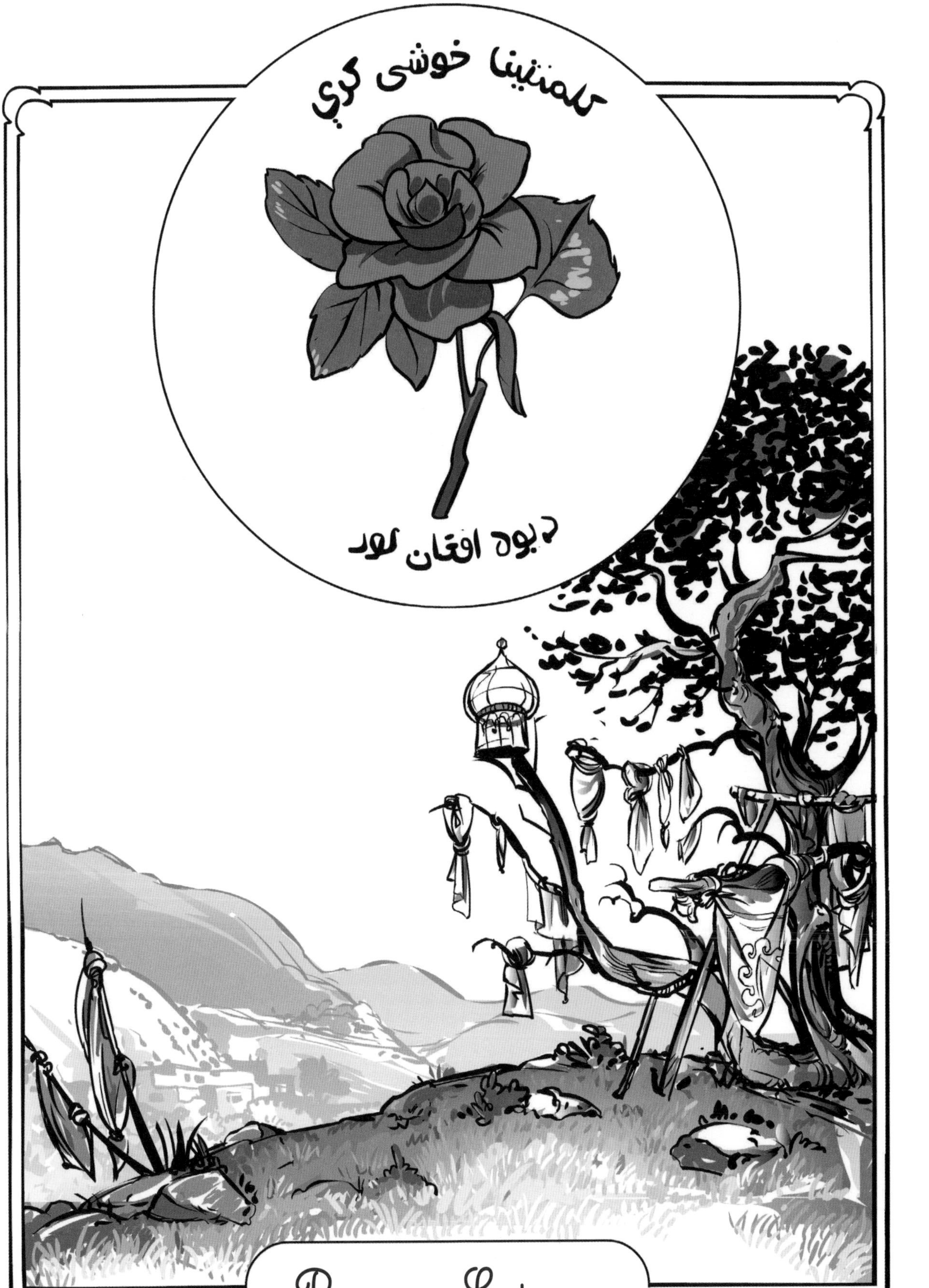
کلمنتینا خوشي کړي
د یوه افغان لور

Bonus Section

THE COVERS FOR THE TEN-VOLUME *YASSIN* & *KAKA RAOUF* SERIES

THE FIRST SIX VOLUMES WERE
COMMISSIONED BY USAID,
AND PLAYFULLY EXPLAIN THE
CONSTITUTION, CIVIL RIGHTS,
AND JUDICIARY REFORMS IN
AFGHANISTAN TODAY. THESE
SMALL COMICS WERE DESIGNED
TO BE UNDERSTANDABLE TO
ILLITERATE PEOPLE, WITH
PICTOGRAMS REPLACING DIALOGUE
BALLOONS (IN 2005, THE COUNTRY
HAD AN 80% ILLITERACY RATE).
READING IS ASSISTED BY
SIDE NOTES IN DARI AND PASHTO
(AFGHANISTAN'S TWO MAIN
LANGUAGES). THE COMICS WERE
INTENDED FOR USE AS TEACHING
AIDS IN PRIMARY AND SECONDARY
SCHOOLS. AROUND 35,000 COPIES
WERE DISTRIBUTED NATIONWIDE,
AND THE TWO MAIN CHARACTERS
BECAME SO POPULAR IN SCHOOL
PLAYGROUNDS THAT USAID MADE
AN ANIMATED ADAPTATION FOR
AFGHAN TELEVISION.

VOLUME SEVEN, COMMISSIONED BY NEW YORK UNIVERSITY, FEATURES THE
SAME CHARACTERS EXPLAINING HOW THE AFGHAN PARLIAMENT OPERATES.
IT CIRCULATED SEVERAL MONTHS BEFORE THE PARLIAMENTARY ELECTIONS,
HELPING YOUNGER READERS GET FAMILIAR WITH THE CONCEPT OF A
LEGISLATURE.

THE LAST THREE VOLUMES IN THE
SERIES, COMMISSIONED BY UNICEF,
DELVE INTO THE RIGHTS OF THOSE
WITH DISABILITIES AND THE RANGE
OF PROBLEMS THEY ENCOUNTER IN
SOCIETY.

IN THIS EPISODE, YASSIN, WHO'S BARELY 14, IS EXPLOITED BY AN EVIL BLACKSMITH, JABBAR. YASSIN MANAGES TO ESCAPE AND CONTACTS THE VILLAGE COUNCIL (KNOWN AS THE SHURA IN AFGHANISTAN). ONE OF THE COUNCIL MEMBERS, KAKA RAOUF, ADOPTS YOUNG YASSIN, THUS RELEASING HIM FROM FORCED LABOR SO HE CAN GO BACK TO SCHOOL. THE TWO ARTICLES HIGHLIGHTED HERE ARE THE PROHIBITION OF CHILD LABOR, AND COMPULSORY EDUCATION FOR CHILDREN.

IN THE SIXTH EPISODE OF THE SERIES, YASSIN AND KAKA RAOUF WANDER AROUND INSIDE A GIANT CONSTITUTION.

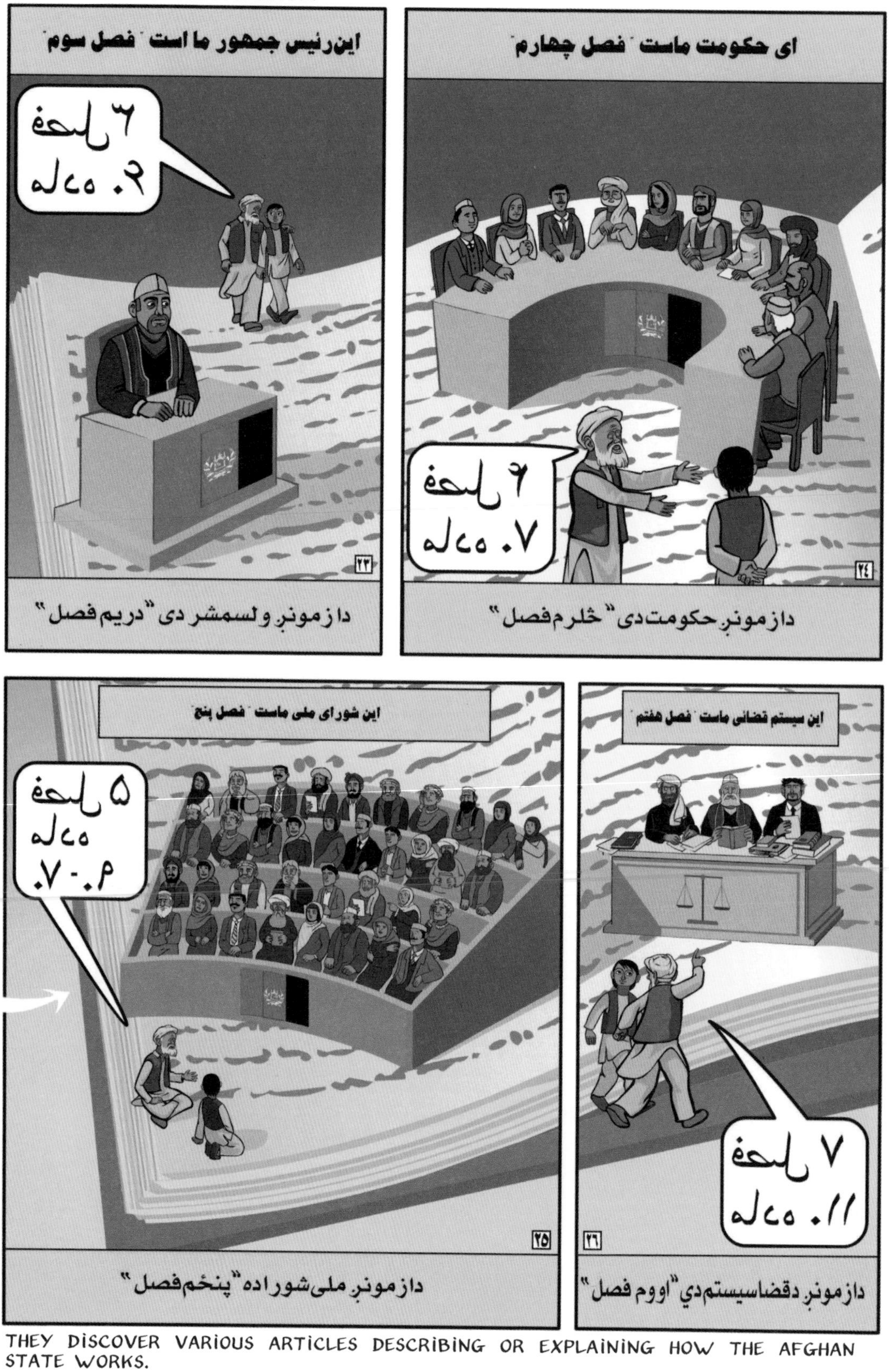

این رئیس جمهور ما است "فصل سوم"
دا زمونږ ولسمشر دی "دریم فصل"
ای حکومت ماست "فصل چهارم"
دازمونږ حکومت دی "څلرم فصل"
این شورای ملی ماست "فصل پنج"
دازمونږ ملی شوراده "پنځم فصل"
این سیستم قضائی ماست "فصل هفتم"
دازمونږ دقضاسیستم دي "اووم فصل"

GOSH! WHAT A LOVELY ILLUSTRATION OF THE AFGHAN PARLIAMENT!

THEY DISCOVER VARIOUS ARTICLES DESCRIBING OR EXPLAINING HOW THE AFGHAN STATE WORKS.

این نظام اداری ماست . فصل هشتم

بیا که پس بریم خانه . چشمهایت را بسته کو

دا زمونږ اداری نظام دی "اتم فصل"

راخه چی کورته ولاړ شو، سترګی دی وتره

چشمهای را باز کو

حالیکه تو قانون اساسی را یاد گرفتی به دیگران یاد بتی

سترګی دی خلاص کړه

اوس چی تا اساسی قانون و پیژندی، نور و ته ئی وپیژنی

NOW THAT YOUR COUNTRY'S CONSTITUTION HOLDS
NO MORE SECRETS FOR YOU, HURRY OFF AND TELL
YOUR CLASSMATES WHAT YOU HAVE LEARNED!

IN ANOTHER EPISODE, YASSIN'S SISTER, AAMENA, RETURNS FROM PAKISTAN WHERE SHE FLED AS A REFUGEE DURING THE WAR. TOGETHER WITH HER BROTHER, SHE TRIES TO FIND THEIR PARENTS' HOUSE. SADLY, A WARLORD HAS SEIZED IT. OUR YOUNG HEROES DO GET IT BACK AT THE END OF THE ISSUE, THANKS TO AN ORDER FROM A COURT SET UP TO RESOLVE SUCH DISPUTES. THE TWO CONSTITUTIONAL ARTICLES ILLUSTRATED HERE ARE THOSE GUARANTEEING PROPERTY RIGHTS.

OUR TWO FRIENDS COME ACROSS A BOY WHO LOST AN ARM AND A LEG WHEN HE STEPPED ON A LANDMINE. THE BOY IS GOOD AT FIXING THINGS, AND FINDS A PLACE IN SOCIETY THANKS TO KAKA RAOUF'S ASSISTANCE AND WISE ADVICE.

IN THIS EPISODE, YASSIN, AAMENA AND KAKA RAOUF VISIT A SCHOOL FOR BLIND AND PARTIALLY SIGHTED GIRLS, WHERE THEY WOULD LIKE TO ENROLL YASSIN'S COUSIN.

AND TO FINISH THE BOOK OFF IN STYLE, SOME SELECTED PHOTOS...

THAT'S ME IN THE MIDDLE, DRESSED UP LIKE A WARLIKE MUJAHIDEEN FOR THE OCCASION. I POSTED THOSE KINDS OF PHOTOS TO MY BLOG TO SCARE MY FAMILY.

WITH TRISTAN IN BAMIYAN. WE SAT UP ON OUR HOTEL ROOF TO DRAW THE CLIFF WITH THE GIANT BUDDHAS.

A BURQA-SELLER DOZING IN HERAT.

PUYA AND JEF BEHIND SERGEANT AZUL'S SUPERBIKE RADIO/UMBRELLA.

20,000 AFGHAN SOLDIERS AND ME AND ME AND ME...

JEF'S ASSISTANT PRACTICES TURRET-WALKING IN THE VALLEY OF LOST TANKS.

AN AFGHAN ARMY BAND PLAYING THE ATTAN-i-MiLi (NATIONAL ANTHEM) FOR OUR IMMENSE ENJOYMENT.

MAUD SAMPLES THE DELIGHTS OF HORSE-RIDING.
HARUN, NATHAN, TRISTAN AND ME RE-ENACTING MANET'S LE DÉJEUNER SUR L'HERBE.

WHAT MORE CAN I SAY?

MY HOUSE...

I FOUND AND DISARMED
OSAMA BIN LADEN.

"GOODBYE, DEAR READERS, AND DON'T FORGET
TO BUY THE NEXT VOLUME OF KABUL DISCO!"

KABUL DISCO

**Book 2 : How I managed not to become
addicted to opium in Afghanistan**

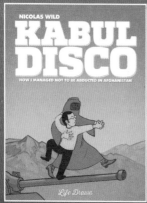
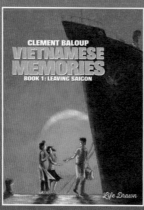